NIGHT

A major new series of original paperbacks. NIGHTSHADES are contemporary novels for women – a new kind of love story.

NIGHTSHADES

NIGHTSHADES

Katie Penhaligan

TICKET TO RIDE

FONTANA PAPERBACKS

First published by Fontana Paperbacks 1983

Copyright © 1983 by Katie Penhaligan

Made and printed in Great Britain by
William Collins Sons & Co. Ltd

FOR KEVIN PERLMUTTER,
WHO MADE IT ALL POSSIBLE

PROLOGUE

The young man lay on the gently sloping grass bank. He lifted his hand to obscure the sun from his eyes and looked at his watch. Nearly an hour and a half had gone by since his call to the A.A. from an isolated house about half a mile down the road. The hand dropped limply, lazily, to his chest to rejoin the other in a comfortable clasp, and the man closed his eyes again and returned to his reverie. It was easy for his thoughts to wander carelessly while the warm English spring sun soothed his face and bathed his daydreams.

He smiled to himself. He supposed it was a bit foolish, even a little contrary to keep the old Mini he'd had for so many years, when he was now in a position to buy virtually any car he desired. But every time something went wrong with it (which was happening with increasing frequency these days) and it seemed that now was time to part with the old banger, in the final analysis he couldn't quite bring himself to do it. And now the offending vehicle stood, with bonnet raised, looking slightly sorry for itself, beside him.

As his thoughts drifted, deep in his consciousness he was becoming aware of a distant, fast ticking sound, getting closer and louder until, suddenly, it stopped.

'Hello.' The young man opened one eye, and on focusing it on the bearer of the greeting, felt immediately compelled to open the other. Before him stood perhaps the prettiest young woman he had ever seen. Was he dreaming? he thought. Had he been even more relaxed than he imagined, and actually dropped off?

She stood astride a bicycle (he realized now what the noise he'd heard had been). She had beautifully thick, shoulder-length blonde hair which was edged and highlighted by the bright sun behind her. The young man judged her to be in her early twenties and she was dressed in the simple casual clothes of her generation, clinging jeans and a loose, billowing navy blue sweatshirt. She wore no make-up, and the lack of it tended to enhance rather than detract from her undeniable natural beauty. The man was momentarily spell-bound. Her fresh complexion, lively, aware eyes and careless smile gave her an almost angelic air which, although it seemed to the man a little unreal, somehow didn't seem out of place with the perfect day and idyllic rural setting. Now he came to think about it, people always did appear more appealing and friendly when the sun shone.

'Well, you've obviously broken down,' said the girl. 'Are you waiting for the R.A.C. or something?'

'The A.A. actually.' The young man scrambled to his feet thinking he should probably have stood up earlier, instead of staring at the girl rather rudely from his supine position on the bank.

'My father belongs to the R.A.C. I think it's the "Royal" aspect of it that appeals to him. He probably thinks it puts him in the running for a knighthood or something.' The girl laughed and the man, who had now composed himself a little, smiled back with growing confidence. He put on a gruff old English colonel's voice.

'No, no. Always been an A.A. man myself. Won't hear a word said against 'em. Wonderful organization.'

'How long have you been waiting?' the girl asked.

'About an hour and a half,' the young man replied rather sheepishly, now with his normal voice. The girl gave another short giggle and the man smiled again. 'Well, not that wonderful, I suppose.'

There was a pause while neither of them seemed quite sure what to say next. She really was exceptionally pretty, thought the young man, and yet not in a distant, inaccessible way. There was an inviting softness and warmth about her that he found unusual in someone he was meeting for the first time.

'Look, I'll tell you what,' said the girl. 'Why don't you give me all the relevant details, and I'll call the A.A. again for you from a phone-box on my way through Radwinter.'

'Yes, thank you. That would be most kind,' said the man. He scribbled his name, address, A.A. membership number and the make and year of his car on an old envelope he found in the glove compartment and handed it to the girl.

The vigilant sun, perched high on its sweeping, panoramic arc over the earth, watched. Silently. Inscrutably. The only witness.

ONE

Sarah Brownlow squeezed past the stooping, dithering passengers as she searched for her seat on the Boeing 747. Eventually finding it, she was pleased to see that at least she wasn't going to be stuck in the centre column with no hope at all of a decent view. However, she was still one seat away from the window where a man sat staring dreamily out of it at the bustling activity on the tarmac. He turned to face her as she struggled into her place and attempted to work out the best way of arranging her hand luggage on the floor by her feet. Sarah looked up for a moment, instinctively aware that he was now observing her. The man looked to be in his early forties, though he wore his light brown hair slightly long, which gave him something of a boyish quality. He was handsome too. She smiled briefly, said 'hello' and returned absently to what was primarily occupying her attention.

Then she stopped and regarded her neighbour again. Because it had suddenly registered on her that the man's expression could only be described as one of extreme shock.

'Is there something wrong?' she remarked, somewhat unsettled by the man's wide-eyed stare.

'Er, no. Not really.' He seemed to shake himself into a more composed state. 'I'm sorry. Please forgive me,' he said. 'I thought for a moment that . . . No. I'm sorry, how rude of me.'

For the first hour or so of the Pan-Am flight from London to New York the two of them didn't speak. Sarah leafed through the glossy magazine she had found in the pocket on the back of the seat in front of her. But out of the corner of her eye she could just catch glimpses of the man beside her, who seemed to be staring at her for long periods. It made her shiver. Sarah smiled nervously at him, once or twice, and eventually they struck up a conversation. The man's name was Andrew Simpson, an Englishman who had settled in Bridgeport, Connecticut twelve years before, immediately after his first visit to the United States.

'I was only there for two weeks, and that was it. I was hooked,' he revealed, as they chatted comfortably, the initial unease now apparently dissipated.

Simpson really had done pretty well for himself in those twelve years. Being a watchmaker by trade, he had had no difficulty getting a job. A skill like that was remarkably useful in America when it came to applying for a work permit and social security number. And then, gradually, over the years he had begun to dabble in buying and selling antiques, making frequent forays into Europe to plunder it of still more valuable relics to satisfy the American wealthy. It was from just such a trip that he was returning now.

Kennedy Airport didn't seem very different to any other Sarah had known. With its stark, clinical, modern architecture and ambience, it represented a bland international sterility that failed to excite her sensibilities. This was no more New York than Heathrow was London, or Orly was Paris.

They shuffled a few inches forward in the slow-moving queue to have their passports checked. Sarah took the opportunity to study Simpson a little more closely while he seemed momentarily preoccupied with the hubbub and movement going on around them. He really was quite attractive, she thought, if a bit on the short side.

'Hey, listen,' Simpson said after a couple of minutes. Then he placed his hand luggage, two carrier bags full of duty free liquor, on the ground between his feet and began rummaging through his jacket pockets. 'Let me give you my address and telephone number.' He began jotting these down on a piece of paper he had torn from the back of a diary. 'And then, if you get a chance to get out to Connecticut, and you want somewhere to stay,' he looked up from his scribblings and smiled mischievously, 'I'm sure something could be arranged.' Sarah suddenly felt very tired. It was something that happened to her often, these days. She would be bubbling and full of life one minute and then, quite out of the blue, the energy would drain from her and she would feel hopelessly listless. And with the tiredness came an irritability which now affected her attitude to Andrew Simpson who, it now seemed quite clear to her, was just like all other men and plainly only after one thing! She almost snatched the scrap of paper from his hand.

'Yes, well thanks. I'll put it on file, or something,' she muttered testily. 'But Connecticut sounds a bit boring to me actually. I shouldn't think I'll bother. Do you mind if I go first?'

They were now standing at the front of their queue, and Sarah, without waiting for the stunned Simpson's reply, strode into the booth ahead of them like a racehorse into the starting stall.

Sarah was met by her cousin Cathy and spouse Frank, which proved to be a more moving experience than she had expected. They all hugged one another with an almost desperate intensity. Sarah and Cathy sobbed uncontrollably, and even the usually calm, cool Frank found it difficult to restrain the tears that threatened to well in his eyes.

It had been two years since Sarah had last seen them. Then Cathy, an American by birth and her delicious new husband, Frank Robson, had visited England for their honeymoon. Cathy, who was six years older than Sarah, had been to England once or twice in recent years. These had been business trips where she would be looking to buy bulk supplies of Liberty and such-like prints for making high-fashion clothes back in the States. For Frank it had been his first trip to 'the old country' as he called it. They'd stayed much of the time with the Brownlows in their large house on the outskirts of Saffron Walden, making frequent journeys into London and sometimes stopping overnight in a hotel.

Sarah remembered long walks through the lovely North Essex countryside. And when in London with them, there would be crazed shopping sprees, lunch at Tuttons and, if they really wanted to indulge themselves, tea at Fortnum and Mason's.

She sighed to herself as she walked with the Robsons to the Chevrolet they had left in the airport car park. That had been almost exactly two years ago, before so much had happened; when life had seemed so much better – so free of some of its appalling and tragic consequences. It had all made their reunion that much more poignant. Her life had changed significantly in that time, and she yearned desperately for the simplicity and warmth that she had come to feel would never be hers again.

Frank and Cathy Robson's apartment was a spacious two-bedroomed affair in an elegant 1930s building on the fashionable upper east side of the city. Frank, an interior designer by profession, had stamped his inimitable style on the place. But Cathy had had her say too, especially when it came to the choice of fabrics for curtains and coverings. The curtains in the sitting room hung imposingly from ceiling to floor, their large, swirling pattern and deep, rich colouring complemented perfectly by the plain, oatmeal carpet and maroon corduroy three-piece suite. The hi-fi took pride of place in the room, stacked one item on top of another to form a monolithic tower of Japanese electronic wizardry. Its clinical, brushed aluminium face provided a sharp contrast to the muted sophistication of some of the other colourings. And when it was in action, its flashing multi-coloured lights resembled a kind of constantly-changing Manhattan skyline. Overall, Cathy and Frank had managed to combine the period attributes of the apartment perfectly with more modern, Hi-Tech ideas. And in doing so, they had successfully created a home which embodied the best aspects of both styles without being an uncoordinated hotch-potch of them. Cathy was a great lover of plants too. They were everywhere. Yuccas, cheese plants, umbrella palms and grape ivies; small ones in beautiful, pastel-coloured art-deco pots could be found on every available flat surface; and tall, noble-looking specimens stood guard on the floor in the corners of most of the rooms.

It was the first time Sarah had been to America, and New York seemed the obvious choice for her initiation. But she had been warned by both Americans and others who knew the country well that although New York was probably the most exciting city in the world, it didn't represent what was to be found in the rest of the United States.

'Once you get outside a one hundred mile radius of it the people and tempo of life change so much, you could be in a completely different country,' Cathy herself had said to her during that last trip to England.

But in the meantime, what was all this fuss about the 'Big Apple'?

June in New York was about to turn languidly into July. It was hot. Up in the low nineties most days. It took Sarah a couple of days to adjust to being pounded by a blast of intensely humid heat each time she left the relative comfort of an air-conditioned building to go outside.

With Cathy and Frank working, Sarah was left very much to her own devices. This suited her. She didn't feel pressurized. She wasn't bombarded with questions about her day each evening. And in turn, Cathy and Frank were happy just to be there when she needed them, without feeling it necessary to lead her, like some mindless tourist, around the usual 'sights'. She would find them out for herself in good time. It was a very satisfactory arrangement. Whatever she wanted to know, they would tell her. But they all agreed that the only way Sarah was going to find out what really made New York tick was to walk and bus around it at her leisure. As long as she kept clear of Harlem and The Bronx, the people were as friendly as anywhere in the world.

13

'It's not like London, you know,' Cathy had said. 'No one in New York feels inhibited or embarrassed about talking to strangers.'

Up and down Manhattan's long straight avenues, woven together by its more numerous, shorter streets, Sarah would walk and walk as much as the heat would allow. And then she'd collapse, exhausted, into a restaurant or coffee bar to cool off and replenish her sagging energy level with something to eat.

Sarah had just come out of Macy's department store into the steaming bustle of 34th Street. Even if they did claim it to be the world's largest store, Sarah for one hadn't been too impressed with it. Waiting ten minutes to pay for a pair of socks, and then being told that they didn't accept *Mastercard* wasn't her idea of the famous American service. So what was she going to do now? She looked at her watch. 11.45. Well, she supposed that could loosely be construed as lunch-time.

She was fast sinking into the American habit of perpetual eating. God, she'd eaten so much since she'd been there. But it was all anyone ever seemed to do in New York. Just about every other shop was a restaurant, coffee bar or food shop of some kind. Still, with all the walking she had been doing it didn't seem to have affected her weight. She had weighed herself that morning on the Robsons' digital scales. 113 pounds. And a not too taxing mental calculation had revealed that she weighed the same eight stone one pound as when she'd left England.

Sarah glanced down the street and caught sight of a man, about fifty yards away, with a rather animated expression on his face, apparently making straight for her. She certainly didn't recognize him at first sight. She briefly imagined that the classic film or T.V. situation would occur where he would dash straight past her into the waiting arms of a girl standing a few yards away. Sarah thought it was funny how, in New York, one always felt they were in a film or slap bang in the middle of an episode of *Kojak*. But there seemed to be no doubt about it. He was heading straight for her.

'My God, I don't believe it. Fancy seeing you again. And in New York of all places.' The man was tall and slim, without being skinny, and he had clear, hazel eyes that had an instant, spell-binding effect on Sarah. They were dazzling. His softly curling dark brown hair and moustache had a slightly red tinge. He was good-looking, too, but it was those wonderful stunning eyes that really stole the show. She reckoned that he was probably in his early thirties. But what surprised her most about him was his English accent.

On the face of it, this didn't appear to be just a casual pick-up attempt. The man's breathlessness and apparently genuine excitement suggested that he really did recognize her. But for the life of her, even though he was now close up and she'd had those extra few seconds to study him, she didn't think she knew him from Adam. But then again, her memory had been one of the things to suffer over the last year. Sometimes she would do something one day and have no recollection of it, whatsoever, the next.

Her blankness was obvious in her expression. 'Surely you haven't forgotten,' he smiled. 'The Saffron Walden–Finchingfield road? About two or three months ago? Broken down Mini? Me waiting for the A.A.? You stop on a bicycle? Offer to call them again for me?' The young man fired the clues at her like a T.V. quiz show compere trying to help her win tonight's star prize.

Well, this is all very strange, Sarah thought. Very strange indeed. It was surely too much of a coincidence. It was certainly true that she did bicycle along that very road sometimes at weekends, when the weather was fine, to visit friends in Little Sampford. Though less so these days, for obvious reasons. It was possible then. Probable in fact.

'I'm afraid I do have *the* most appalling memory. But I think you must be right. My family live in Saffron Walden and, well,' she shrugged nervously, 'I'm around there a lot of the time.'

The young man laughed.

'I'm afraid the chap from the A.A. who eventually came said that my first call was the only one they'd received.'

'Oh,' said Sarah, slightly bewildered. She forced a nervous laugh as a bizarre thought jarred in her mind. She shivered in an attempt to dislodge its unthinkable implications, and the feeling of unease that had suddenly descended upon her lifted.

'Er . . . look,' said the young man as he glanced, now seeming slightly embarrassed, down at his shoes. 'I hope you don't think I'm trying to pick you up or anything. But . . .' He looked up at her again. '. . . How do you feel about grabbing a small bite to eat?'

Sarah found herself amused and curiously drawn by the young man's apparent shyness once the excitement of rediscovering her had worn off. He was really quite nice. And, of course, he was English. It would be nice to talk with a fellow countryman for a time.

'Well, why not?' she smiled. 'I was just about to get a snack somewhere anyway.' They started walking towards Herald Square. 'My name's Sarah. Sarah Brownlow.'

'Mine is – er . . .' The young man looked embarrassed again. Did his name sound so ridiculous that he could hardly bring himself to tell her? '. . . David.'

Oh dear. Well if he wasn't going to be any more forthcoming than that, then this obviously wasn't going to be the chance meeting to change her life.

They didn't have to walk very far before they found a branch of the *Chock Full o' Nuts* coffee bar chain. They went in and sat down at one of its U-shaped bars. Sarah ordered a chicken sandwich and a chocolate milk-shake, while David satisfied himself with a roast beef sandwich and the glass of water placed automatically on the counter as they had sat down.

There was an awkward silence as they waited for the sandwiches to come along. 'What do you do, David?' Sarah ventured. She sighed, a little impatiently, to herself. She considered herself fairly liberated. She didn't believe that it was up to the man to make all the running. But this was beginning to look a little bit like hard work.

'I'm a writer, actually,' David replied.

Oh dear. Not another penniless poet, or mediocre, pretentious wordsmith trying to write the Great British Novel.

'Oh, how absolutely fascinating.' She put on her absolutely fascinated expression, which involved screwing up her forehead and narrowing her eyes slightly. 'Do tell me more. What are you working on at the moment? And by the way, what *is* your surname, if it's not too much to ask? It's just that, well, when you're famous, I can tell people that I met you once outside Macy's in New York.' She giggled.

The young man looked at her, almost apologetically.

'Dent. My name is David Dent.'

Sarah began choking on a mouthful of her sandwich. Her companion had to thump her, heartily, on the back, and she needed to take a long cool draw of her milk-shake before she had recovered herself again. She stared at him, amazed.

'My God. You're not going to tell me you're *the* David Dent. David Dent the bestselling novelist? *The Defector* and all that?' David winced visibly, and looked even more embarrassed.

'I'm afraid so,' he said.

'Oh, what an idiot I am. A fat-headed idiot,' Sarah sighed. 'How can you possibly forgive my rudeness. My . . . my smug assumptions.' She wanted a hole in the ground to open up, for her to disappear into. 'It's just that . . . well, you don't really expect to bump into someone as famous as you, just like that, and end up having a chicken sandwich with him.'

David shook his head.

'Please don't apologize,' he said kindly. 'I'm just glad to have the introductions over and done with. It's all so embarrassing. Anyway now we can act like two ordinary people again.'

But Sarah wasn't going to let it rest as easily as that.

'I must admit, I've never read either of your books. But I saw the film of *The Defector*. I thought it was really good.'

David smiled. Not complacently, but as though he was genuinely amused.

'You don't have to say that, you know. I thought it was pretty terrible actually. Not at all the way I envisaged it.'

'But you wrote the screenplay, didn't you?' said Sarah, feeling a little more at ease.

'Yes, that's right. I did. But I didn't have much say over the rest of it. I don't think the director and I were on quite the same wavelength.'

They chatted on with an ease which belied their relative unfamiliarity, completely oblivious to the time slipping effortlessly by. Sarah told David a little about herself. About Cambridge too and how, in October, she was to start the final year of her English degree.

'I should probably be swotting away in the library at College at this very moment,' she said. And then she went on to tell him how she had made the superficial gesture of bringing a handful of books with her. But a glance at titles like Hobbes' *Leviathan* and Hume's *A Treatise of Human Nature*, as she had unpacked, confirmed to her that their inclusion had not been desperately serious. Then she told David about Cathy and Frank and how she was going to be in New York until late September.

In turn, David revealed that he had only been in the country for a few days. He intended to remain for about a month and was staying in a rented apartment by the Hudson, on Riverside Drive.

He was there primarily because of his next novel, the synopsis for which was causing considerable consternation among his various publishers on both sides of the Atlantic. It was a complete departure from the espionage themes of his first two books and, as such, horrified all those publishers and agents who stood to make a lot of money from the continuation of a winning formula. So David was in New York to talk the subject over with his American publishers and have a long, serious think about it for himself. He could also do with a holiday. He had only ever known New York fleetingly, often stopping off merely for a few days which would be filled with meetings and press or television interviews. He had never got a really good look at the city.

Prompted by Sarah's questioning, David told her how he had started his writing career, writing both his novels in his spare time, while an underpaid reporter on a local paper in Bishop's Stortford. In fact it was not much more than a year ago that success had enabled him to finally give up his job and write full-time.

'Writing the first one, *The Defector*, was great fun. It was a bit of a challenge. And that's something I can never resist.' David ordered another milk-shake for Sarah, and decided to have one for himself as well. 'But *Chain Reaction* was much harder. I suppose I got a bit big-headed. But I couldn't come to terms with the fact that there I was, the author of a pretty successful spy novel, although the film hadn't come out at that time, and yet I was having to do the second one in between reporting on local cricket matches and flower shows.'

Sarah gave a short burst of laughter.

But *Chain Reaction* had proved even more successful than

The Defector, and a film based on it was going through its casting phase at the moment.

Sarah remembered reading articles about David Dent, although she'd never seen a photograph of him. *The Times* had called him things like 'the best writer of espionage fiction since Graham Greene and John le Carré'. As she admitted, she had never read either of his books, but she got the impression, from others and from what she'd read about him, that he was a highly respected writer as well as being a commercially successful one. And that was a combination which it seemed could only be achieved by very special novelists.

And yet there didn't seem to be anything big-headed about David Dent. There wasn't the slightest element of swagger or conceit in his manner or the way he spoke. In fact he was remarkably reticent for one so prominently in the public eye. Almost embarrassed to be who he was. He was quite good-looking, Sarah observed, without being stunningly handsome. But he had a warmth and humour which drew her invitingly to explore beneath the superficial facade of appearances. It excited her. She couldn't quite put her finger on it. All she knew was that she felt both contented and surprisingly elated in his company.

It wasn't until they had parted at around two o'clock after she had agreed to have dinner with him that evening, and she had strolled slowly back to the Robsons' apartment and was standing naked beneath the cooling gush of the shower, that she began to sense a very definite tingle of anticipation.

TWO

Sarah dozed contentedly on the bed. Clad loosely in her pale blue towelling bathrobe, she lay, floating deliciously between the fathomless world of dreams and the reality of the distantly buzzing traffic outside. Her half-sleeping, half-wakeful mind flitted randomly from one indulgent thought to another.

And she *was* looking forward to her evening with David Dent. Her shower had been wonderfully refreshing, and her little doze afterwards had left her feeling relaxed but alert. She swung her legs off the bed and stood up. A couple of paces and she was in view of the full-length mirror fixed to the door of the room. A fleeting wave of fear came over her as she focused her gaze on her reflection. She still, even now, found it difficult to summon the courage to look at herself. Vivid images of what she used to see flashed through her mind's eye: hideous representations of uncontrolled obesity – the cruel tricks of a mind tormented by *anorexia nervosa*. It had been just one of the mental strains she had been forced to endure over the last year. She had never been overweight in her life, and yet, what with the pressures of everything else as well, she had suddenly found herself convinced that she was.

But now there was no such distortion of the truth before her. Sarah untied the belt of her bathrobe and allowed it to fall open. She smiled appreciatively as she ran her hands down her breasts to her waist and, finally, to her thighs.

Not bad, she thought, half-surprised. Not bad at all.

A confidence that she had forgotten could exist had crept up on her gradually, even warily. But it was there nonetheless, its warmth and certainty slowly coursing through her veins, nerves and muscles. She could feel it.

Sarah tied up her bathrobe again. 'I'm hungry,' she said to herself. 'And I know just what I fancy.' She strode determinedly into the kitchen and began opening and closing cupboards until she found what she was looking for: a can of baked beans. She placed it under the wall-mounted electric can-opener and let the contraption do its job. 'I haven't done this for years,' she murmured as she felt around the cutlery drawer for a dessert spoon.

'Mmm, delicious.' The first mouthful brought with it familiar echoes of her childhood. Cold baked beans straight out of the can had been one of her biggest weaknesses until only a few years before.

'Yuk,' Penny used to say. And she'd shake her head disgustedly. 'How could you? They're bad enough hot. But cold . . . ?'

Penny. Penny. Sarah sighed to herself. Her mind was drifting again. 'What do you think of him, Penny? David Dent, I mean. I wish you could tell me.' She strolled into the sitting room, and over to the window that overlooked the street.

Although it was getting on for five o'clock, the street a couple of storeys below wasn't particularly busy. The occasional car or small truck would cruise by, but most of the traffic was hammering relentlessly along nearby Third Avenue. The sun, though hazy, was still strong, but such shadows as existed, were just perceptibly beginning to lengthen.

Sarah took another mouthful of beans. They really were refreshing in this kind of weather, she thought.

There weren't many people in the street. Those that were there moved along slowly and deliberately in the heat. A dog dozed contentedly on the other side in the shadow of one of the apartment blocks, too drowsy and sun-baked to bother chasing a fat ginger cat that seemed intent on pestering him. Sarah's glance moved idly from this little scene and fixed itself on the back of a young woman leaning lazily against a lamp-post.

The girl had long straight blonde hair, rather like Sarah's own, and a slim petite figure. She wore tight-fitting jeans and a navy blue sweatshirt. She didn't seem to be doing anything, except standing there. But Sarah couldn't see what she looked like because she was facing the other way.

She was just about to turn away from the window and dispose of the now empty baked bean can in her hand, when the girl suddenly turned round and looked directly up at her. Sarah couldn't move. Couldn't do anything. She tried to make a sound, but nothing would come out. She felt every hair on her body tingle and bristle, and her face burned. The empty can slipped uncontrollably from her hand and she slid down the wall to the floor. Then it came. The scream. The high-pitched scream that was both a relief and a comfort.

'Sarah. My God, what the hell is the matter?' Frank stood in the open doorway, a strong and welcome presence. He rushed over to where she sat, staring into space, propped against the wall. He squatted beside her and enveloped her with his powerful, protective arms.

'Hey, honey. Come on, what is it?' He spoke in a low, soothing tone.

What could she say? Sarah wondered. How could she put that appalling vision into words that Frank would believe or understand? How could she tell him that she had just seen her sister Penny outside? But Penny had been dead for over a year.

Until the previous year, Sarah and Penny Brownlow had been inseparable. They had almost lived each other's lives. Throughout an idyllic shared childhood, scampering about the rooms of the large, sprawling old family house in Essex; through school and the pains and joys of adolescence; first loves and loves lost; tears of laughter and tears of sorrow. But together. Always together. Until that unbelievable April day when the world seemed to stop.

The effect of Penny's tragic death on the Brownlow family was predictably shattering; for Sarah in particular. For weeks she refused to believe it had happened. In her state of acute shock and with her total inability to accept the truth she bitterly blamed her parents for admitting to the fact that Penny wasn't with them any more. And never would be.

Then came the emptiness. The big, gaping hole in her soul. A dark, fathomless abyss that was just . . . nothing. The hallucinations and anorexic tendencies were just two of the by-products of a breakdown that the best psychiatrists in London were at a loss to analyse and treat. In the end it seemed that time, in its slow yet assured way, had begun to silently, diligently knit her fragmented mind together again. The New York trip was to be a kind of convalescence for Sarah. An extended period away from home and its echoes of the past was, everyone considered, a good thing for her. But now it seemed that perhaps those echoes hadn't been left back in England after all. They were whirling in their erratic, confused dance around Sarah's mind. Teasing her. Taunting her. Trying to keep her broken.

She must keep it to herself, she thought. She was supposed to have virtually recovered, and neither Frank, nor Cathy for that matter, should be made to worry about her. Now the initial shock had worn off, she felt somewhat better. She had come to her senses. She couldn't really have seen Penny – it must have been someone who looked very like her. But it had not – could not – have been her sister.

Sarah raised her head, her mind working overtime in the quest for a believable excuse for her extraordinary behaviour. It came at just the right moment. Simple.

'Oh, I'm such a fool.' She gave a nervous laugh that she hoped was convincing. 'There was a spider crawling up the window as I was looking out. And there's nothing I detest more than spiders. I absolutely loathe them. They just seem to have that paralysing effect on me. Ugh.' And she shivered. She didn't like lying to Frank, at all. But in these circumstances Sarah felt it was necessary. For now, anyway. Frank smiled.

'Is that all?' he said. Sarah smiled too.

'Frank, what's the time?' she said with a new animation which she hoped didn't seem contrived.

Frank looked at his watch.

'It's nearly five-thirty,' he replied, a little surprised at her sudden change of mood. 'Cathy should be home any time now. Why, are you doing something this evening?'

Sarah winked and clicked her tongue.

'Yup. Sure am.' She affected a thick southern drawl.

'The suspense is killing me. Do you want to tell me, or is this guessing game time?'

'I've got a date, actually.' Sarah rocked her head from side to side with a feigned cockiness. 'And you'll never guess who it is. Never in a million years.'

Frank stood up and winced from the momentary spasm of cramp that shot through the back of his right leg.

'Dustin Hoffman.'

'Huh. You can mock, Frank Robson. I don't suppose you've ever heard of *The Defector* or *Chain Reaction*, have you?'

Sarah enjoyed the playful bantering with Frank. In the week she had been there she had already found that they shared a similar sense of humour, and could go on for hours teasing one another relentlessly in conversations that poor Cathy often found quite beyond her. And Frank, for his part, was happy now to make the most of the welcome change in Sarah's mood by playing along with her.

'Sure I've heard of them,' he smiled. 'I wouldn't be caught dead reading them, though. Too complicated and involved for me, I'm afraid. No, give me Harold Robbins every time. That's my idea of a good escapist read.'

'But do you know who wrote them?' Sarah asked, raising her eyebrows.

'Yeah. Guy called Dent, wasn't it? David Dent, I think.' Frank turned and strolled lazily into the kitchen, easing loose his shoes and kicking them off onto the floor on his way. Then he turned, came out into the sitting room again, and crossed his arms. He looked at Sarah with his head cocked to one side. 'You're not going to tell me you're going out with him.'

Sarah faced him and mockingly copied his stance.

'Could be.'

'Where did you meet him, for Chrissakes?'

'In the street.' Sarah smirked.

'In the street?' Frank shook his head. 'So if a guy stopped you in Central Park, said his name was Ronald Reagan and asked you out to dinner, you wouldn't think it a little odd?'

'Well, he's picking me up at seven.'

'David Dent is coming here, to this apartment, at seven o'clock? Are you crazy?'

'He certainly is. Do you fancy trying to call my bluff?'

'Oh, Jesus. And look at the state of this place.' Frank picked up the shoes he'd kicked off and scurried into the bedroom, muttering to himself. Sarah giggled, and as she did so she heard the key turn in the lock. That must be Cathy, she thought.

THREE

Sarah and David got to Maxwell's Plum restaurant on First Avenue just after seven-thirty. Frank had predicted that they would have to wait some time for their various courses. 'I've seen them carry emaciated corpses out from there,' he'd joked. 'You know, people who've had to wait a couple of weeks for their venison, and just couldn't hang on long enough.' Nevertheless, Sarah ignored Frank's warning and ordered the venison. And extremely good it was, too. David ordered the duck, and it was quite obvious to Sarah that he thought it delicious. But far from being aware of the time it took them to get served, the four hours there passed as easily and fluidly as sand through an hour-glass. Even more than at their first meeting earlier in the day, conversation flowed with a comfort and relaxation which belied the briefness of their acquaintance.

Sarah chatted about her home in Saffron Walden and her parents.

'Daddy's an inventor,' she said. 'He conceives all sorts of weird agricultural contraptions, and spends days on end in his old study making sketches and calculations, and things. We don't usually understand what he's doing, though. And Mummy just humours him, in between making jam and going to W.I. meetings.'

Then David spoke about his own parents. He was obviously quite proud of the fact that his roots were working class. His mother and father had worked hard all their lives. But with David as their only child, they had been determined that he should have the best possible education they could afford. Fortunately they were helped by the fact that David was a very bright boy. He won a much sought-after scholarship to the Leys School in Cambridge, and then

27

sailed into Magdalen College, Oxford, with no difficulty whatever. But he had done it all with hard work, talent and his parents' encouragement and love. 'I used to despise all those brainless, obnoxious hooray-Henrys at Oxford,' he said, as the waiter brought their second round of coffee. 'It really was a case of more money than sense.' And since then, it seemed, David had harboured an underlying, slow-burning disregard for anyone whose wealth diminished their appreciation of what were, for others, the hard-won successes of life.

Sarah asked David more questions about his work and his background. This had a dual purpose. There was no doubt that she was absorbed by what he had to say. But she also wanted every possible opportunity to listen to his voice. There was something almost hypnotic in its tone.

'What's your new book about?' she asked.

For a moment David looked a trifle uncomfortable, and Sarah noticed that his attractive smile disappeared for an instant. But almost as immediately he recovered himself and the smile returned.

'Well, this might seem a little bit silly to you. But I have this sort of pact with myself.' He took a sip of his coffee. 'I don't actually tell anyone about a work in progress except my publishers and agent. I suppose that must sound awfully conceited. After all, who gives a damn, you're probably thinking? Well, it isn't that at all, really. In fact quite the opposite. It's the lack of confidence that the thing will ever come to fruition that makes me want to keep quiet about it until it does.' He caught the waiter's attention and indicated that they would like some more liqueurs. 'Oh, I tell a lie. There is someone else who knows all about anything I'm working on. Dickens.'

'Dickens?' Sarah asked, puzzled.

'My dog. Dickens is a pedigree Staffordshire bull terrier. Bit of a runt, I'm afraid. And he's getting on a bit. I read everything to him. And if he doesn't like something

I've written, he gets depressed for days, and ignores me.'

Sarah went on to tell him about the pair of basset hounds her parents owned. And from there the conversation had drifted easily and casually onto some other subject, and she had quite forgotten about David's evasiveness concerning his new book, his reason for which she had not found totally convincing.

Their talk revealed a whole host of shared interests. Whether they discussed music, films, art or literature, one of them would mention the name of a rock band, director, artist or book that would send the other into excited cries of recognition and pleasure.

Sarah was having a wonderful time. She felt a warmth and confidence in David's company which made her feel as though she had always known him. As if he had always been part of her life. Of course it's probably the wine, she thought to herself. But when she felt David reach across and take her hand, her heart leapt with a suddenness that quite made her jump. And then, simultaneously they looked up at each other. And Sarah knew in that short, timeless moment that there was something more potent than the wine at work.

Arm in arm they walked. Slowly. Dreamily. Not anywhere in particular, although they unconsciously found themselves heading uptown, in the direction of Cathy and Frank's apartment. And now the animated chatter during dinner had turned to a spell-binding, powerful silence, heavy with the feelings and emotions that words seemed too inadequate to evoke.

Could it be that something truly special was happening to her? she pondered. She'd had romances in the past, but mostly she had flitted through them without them ever touching much deeper than a superficial sense of physical attraction. But somehow, with David it was different. These were the early stages, she knew. But the sweet, smooth night air, the distant echoes of their lively dinner-table conversation still ringing in her ears, and simply David's strong, sure, comforting presence beside her now, all contrived to convince Sarah that she was falling in love.

Eventually they began to discuss what they would do the following day. Already in Sarah's mind and, she assumed, in David's too, there was no doubt whatsoever that they were going to be seeing quite a lot of each other. Nothing had to be said. She just knew it. She knew it with the same certainty as though it had already happened.

'Look. Why don't we give the Met a good going over tomorrow?' said David as they turned off Third Avenue into 73rd Street, where the Robsons' apartment was situated. 'And then, if we've got time we could look in at the Guggenheim. It's only a few blocks further up.'

'Great idea,' Sarah agreed.

They reached the door outside the apartment building and Sarah suddenly realized that she had no idea what was going to happen next. Everything till now had been so sure and positive. Now, a momentary uncertainty hung over them. Perhaps for now, she thought, the best thing to do would be the polite one.

'Er, would you like to come in for a cup of coffee?' she suggested tentatively.

'This may seem a bit crazy,' he said. She noticed the slight frown on David's forehead as he searched for the right words for what he wanted to say. 'I'm not completely sure what you think about tonight.' Sarah made as if to protest and David placed a finger softly over her lips to silence her. 'I *think* I know. But perhaps that's the same as really knowing. I've never been quite sure. But one thing is certain. For me, something very special has happened tonight. It's something which I honestly believe has never occurred for me with such intensity. These things probably sound like terrible clichés, but I don't care. If they're the best words to describe what I think and feel, then I'm not ashamed to use them.' He pulled her to him, and their heads nestled snugly

30

against each other. 'If you get to know me better, I think you'll find that I always try to say exactly what I mean. It's my way of living as close to truth as I possibly can.' He laughed. 'It's funny. I'm a writer of fiction, and yet more truth, more human truth, goes into my work than the whole *Encyclopaedia Britannica*.' David pulled his head away and looked thoughtfully into Sarah's eyes. 'What I'm trying to say to you is that I don't want to break tonight's spell. Not yet, anyway. I want to savour it. Cathy and Frank are great. But I want to go to sleep tonight with my thoughts full of you. Because they *are* full of you. And until the morning there's no room for anyone else.' He leant forward and kissed her lips so delicately that the contact was almost imperceptible. 'I'll be here in the morning,' he whispered. 'At ten.' Then he turned, raised his hand slowly in a gesture of farewell, and wandered off down the street.

Sarah stood there for several minutes, staring after him, until he disappeared from her view. She didn't quite know why, but tears trickled slowly over the contours of her cheeks. Were they happy tears, or sad ones? They seemed to be both. And yet neither. The reason for them was indefinable, just like the knot she felt somewhere inside her, and the sensation flooding through her body that both burned and warmed her simultaneously. Yes, David was right. Let the spell remain unbroken until morning. And tomorrow there would be more magic.

Sarah let herself silently into the apartment. And five minutes later she was in bed asleep, and dreaming.

Sarah sat sipping her morning coffee, while she waited for David to arrive, and tried to piece together remembered fragments from the previous evening's conversations. David's secretiveness about his new book, or whatever he was working on, did strike her as slightly odd. Still, she thought, it's not as if after one day I can consider myself his great confidante. Maybe she would question him about it again sometime. There was no hurry. But she was curious nonetheless.

Sarah hadn't seen Cathy and Frank that morning. As was usually the case, they had left the apartment a good half-hour before she woke up.

She smiled to herself. They were lovely people, Cathy and Frank. Cathy, so sure and sincere. So loving and wise. The perfect match for Frank whose playful forays into cynicism never really did much to hide his soft, caring heart. They were very much in love with each other. That was clear to Sarah. They were never continually smothering each other in kisses and cuddles. But she would occasionally catch glimpses of momentary glances between them that revealed more about their feelings for one another than any overt physical contact. Theirs was an unspoken love, more solid and sure than words could probably imply. And Sarah loved them all the more because of it.

But what about David? As the time crept on towards ten o'clock, she began to grow nervous. Would it be different this morning? Had the special atmosphere died with the moonlight? When she saw him, would she still feel something of what she'd felt as he'd turned and walked away from her? It had only been hours before. But it seemed like a lifetime.

The doorbell rang and shook Sarah out of her reverie. She went over to the entry-phone and picked it up.

'Hello?' she said.

'Hello. It's me.' Sarah knew instantly the magic was still there.

'It's frightening.' Sarah was staring in awe at the floor plan, as they stood in the Great Hall of the Metropolitan Museum of Art. She looked up at David and shook her head. 'We're never going to be able to take it all in on one visit.'

David looked over her shoulder at the plan and scratched his head.

'Mm, I think you're right. I had no idea there was so much here.' He clapped his hands together to help concentrate his mind on a more positive approach to the situation. 'Well, look. Let's not rush it. We'll take it easy. See what we can, and come back another time.'

The Egyptian Wing; the Sackler Wing; the American Wing; the Lehman Pavilion. Paintings; sculptures; musical instruments; furniture; jewellery. The list of exhibits seemed endless. And even with an hour's break over a snack in the grand, sparkling cafeteria, Sarah's head was beginning to swim from its immersion into so much rich and wonderful culture.

It was just before 4.30 when the two of them emerged from the building, hand in hand, and both a little numb from their experience. A mime artist was giving an enchanting performance to the people who sat on the steps that cascaded elegantly down to street level.

Sarah and David made their careful way down the steps, delicately stepping over camera-clad tourists and students in faded Levi's and checked lumberjack shirts, who squatted and sprawled lazily in the sunshine. By this time it was too late to venture inside the Guggenheim Museum. They strolled up Fifth Avenue towards it with the lushly verdant Central Park to their left and the imposingly opulent apartment blocks and public buildings to the right. And as its strange and beautiful shape came properly into view, they both stopped, and were reverentially silent for a moment. Then David said:

'You know, Frank Lloyd Wright hated New York. He said it should be razed to the ground and started all over again. So he designed this place. I suppose he sort of wanted to lead the way.'

Sarah looked down at the pocket-sized New York guide she'd brought with her from England.

'It says here that the interior is even more wonderful. And that people often find it more interesting than the artworks themselves.' She looked up at David. 'We will come back won't we?'

He held her face in his hands and kissed her gently on the end of her nose.

'Of course we will,' he said.

They carried on up Fifth Avenue for six or seven more blocks and then turned into Central Park, and wound their way westwards over to the other side. David had suggested that they buy some food, take it back to his apartment and he would attempt to cook Sarah a meal.

David's rented apartment on Riverside Drive was spacious and elegant. The high ceilings, large panelled doors and beautiful antique furniture gave the place a grand and historical air. David had turned up his nose and claimed that it wasn't really his style. He found it all a little cold. Not very homely. But he couldn't really complain. After all, he wasn't having to pay for it. It was all joint courtesy of his American publisher and the film company who were going to make the movie of *Chain Reaction*.

'It seems they think that all this,' he gestured casually with his hand, 'will somehow make an Englishman feel at home.'

Sarah, though, was very impressed with it. She looked up appreciatively at the elaborate cornices.

'I don't know,' she said. 'I think it's all very nice.'

David put his arms around her and squeezed her close to him.

'Well I'm glad somebody likes it,' he said. 'Now. I'm going to attempt to cook something that won't completely embarrass me. The T.V.'s there if you want it. Or you can come and talk to me while I weave my own brand of culinary magic in the kitchen.'

They eventually sat down to eat at about 7.30. The oeufs en cocotte were a delight and the risotto Milanese that followed, far from being an embarrassment, was delicious and filling. They had also bought two litres of Californian red wine, and by 9.30 they were well over half way through the second one. Sarah began to feel herself floating off into a light and relaxed contentment. They talked even more about themselves. It seemed amazing to Sarah. They had so much to say to one another. David told her about the cottage in Finchingfield, where he lived with Dickens and did all his writing, and more about his parents, who lived in Cambridge, and were now retired. About his ambitions and his speculations on the shape the rest of his life might take.

The topic that Sarah particularly dreaded when talking to anyone these days, who didn't know her very well, had briefly reared its head the previous evening. Inevitably David had asked whether she had any brothers or sisters. She had given her usual negative reply. After all, it was the truth . . . almost. And it avoided complicated explanations and general embarrassment all round. But she had suffered a slight pang of guilt afterwards. She almost wished she had told him the whole story. It was strange. Here was a man, whom she hardly knew, and she felt she wanted to tell him everything about herself. All her secrets. And her thoughts, and hopes, and wishes. Just like the secrets she used to share with Penny. There had been no one like that in her life since Penny. But for the time being, anyway, she would let sleeping dogs lie. The wine may have loosened her tongue. But it had also created the same special atmosphere that had enveloped them the night before, and Sarah didn't want to risk spoiling it. She hoped there would be plenty of time to tell David the truth. And if it happened that there wasn't, then it wouldn't matter, anyway. But as she gazed into those bright hazel eyes of his, she felt her whole body tingle. As in the previous evening, she had an inkling that it wasn't just the wine which made her think they had all the time in the world.

'Okay, let's get these dishes and things cleared away. Then we can relax and watch some television,' David said as he stood up and began piling up the dirty plates and dishes.

Sarah gave him a hand, and they soon transferred everything into the kitchen.

'You like television a lot don't you?' said Sarah inquisitively.

'Yes, I do. Especially American T.V. You see, it never claims to be anything it's not. It's just one-hundred-miles-an-hour entertainment. Pure and simple. You take it or leave it. There's always a thing called an on/off switch. British television really annoys me sometimes. It's always trying to be all things to all men. You get *Coronation Street* followed immediately by some heavy political discussion, and things like that.'

'But isn't that called variety, David?'

David was clearly excited at the prospect of climbing aboard one of his favourite hobbyhorses.

'Yes. But it isn't the kind of variety that people want to switch their minds off to after a hard day's work.'

Sarah frowned slightly and screwed up her face.

'Mm. Well I'm afraid I have to disagree with you. Your argument about the on/off switch applies just the same in Britain, you know.'

'Yes, but it's a question of attitudes. In America most of the television is pulp. And that's absolutely fine.' David was getting quite animated. 'It doesn't pretend to be anything else. If you want to be educated or entertained in a more high-brow way, there are channels just for that. And cable too.'

'Aren't you forgetting that in England we've only got four channels, compared to God knows how many here? And two of those are dedicated to the more, shall we say, esoteric programmes,' Sarah said.

'So what's stopping them having more?' David prodded the air aggressively with his forefinger. 'For God's sake. Look how long it took them to get a fourth channel.'

'Money, David. You've virtually said yourself that America is a television-orientated society. The whole place revolves around that box. There's so much money in it that it's able to perpetuate itself.'

David gave a heavy sigh.

'All right, all right,' he snapped. 'It's just that the British can be so damned small-minded.' His face was set in an expression of sulky resignation, like a small boy, deprived of a favourite toy. Sarah couldn't help smiling. She lifted her arms and draped them around his neck. Nothing could be allowed to destroy the newly found magic between them both.

'Hey, come on,' she pouted. 'You wouldn't want me not saying what I really thought, would you?'

David placed his hands gently on her waist, and smiled, his flash of anger forgotten now, as though it had never occurred.

'I'm sorry. You're right. I'd probably hate you for it,' he whispered. 'But as it is . . . I think I'm probably falling in love with you, instead.'

She had only dared speculate in her thoughts that this might be so. But to hear David actually say it, was something that had, strangely, taken her by surprise. He moved his hands to either side of her face and pulled it close to his. Then he kissed her. First with a gentleness that made her melt, and then with a passion and intensity that she responded to with an equally ferocious voracity. She wanted him. God, how she wanted him. To feel his strength and confidence coursing through her. And yet, in a way, its power frightened Sarah a little. She didn't feel in control of what was happening. But it seemed that David did. For him the time was right, the time was now. He took her by the hand, led her into the bedroom, and closed the door.

They made love, she couldn't remember how many times. All she knew was that each time was better, more fulfilling than the last. David was a wonderful lover – gentle and tender, yet refreshingly dominant by turns. And Sarah felt sure and confident enough to abandon herself completely to him. To be consumed by him to such an extent that they were no longer two people, but one.

David looked at his watch, which he had placed on the small cupboard beside the bed.

'It's almost two o'clock, I suppose you know what that means, don't you?' said David. And Sarah thought he looked quite serious for a moment.

'No, what does it mean?' she replied a little uneasily.

David's face creased into a wide grin, as he leant across and softly kissed her neck.

'It means that we've still got the rest of the night.'

FOUR

For Sarah, the following week was almost a dream. She glided through it, glowing with a radiance that the people around her could not help but notice. She and David were together continuously, hardly out of each other's sight. During the day-time they would brave the some-times unbearable humidity and hungrily devour as many tourist sights as they possibly could.

'I want to be a plain old mindless tourist for a week,' David had said.

But in the evenings the *other* New York took over their entertainment. Greenwich Village throbbed to the frenetic pulse of young New Yorkers enjoying themselves with the same determined enthusiasm that seemed to dominate their working lives, while Little Italy with its non-stop carnival atmosphere, and Chinatown with its pa-goda-shaped pay-phones and oriental policemen, beat the rhythms of their respective cultures with uncanny authen-ticity.

Tirelessly, Sarah and David drifted from jazz club to cinema to restaurant to cocktail bar. Generally just the two of them, but occasionally accompanied by Cathy and Frank. And each time, in the early hours of the morning, they would take a cab back to David's apartment, fall into bed and then suddenly be charged with a new surge of energy. Love's power, again. It would flow between them with an unbridled intensity that brought Sarah to ever-increasing heights of sexual ecstasy. And then she would drift off into a contented, sated slumber, entwined in an inextricable love-knot with David. Her David. The David who was beginning to make her a whole person again.

A week after their first meeting Sarah awoke early in the morning with a start. It wasn't a deep, contented sleep that she was roused from, but a strange and disturbing dream. She glanced at the watch which she had forgotten to remove from her wrist. Four-thirty. I can only have been asleep for about an hour, she thought. She sat up in bed, while David lay beside her, peacefully breathing the heavy air of the sleeper. Wide awake now, she pieced together the fragments of her dream. It didn't take too much effort. The details were stark and vivid in her mind. A man, a youngish man with dark curly hair and a moustache, sat on a grass bank beside a car, on a quiet country road. The car had the bonnet raised. A girl with long blonde hair, wearing a dark baggy sweatshirt and tight-fitting jeans, cruised onto the scene on a bicycle and stopped. They talked for a short time. How long? A minute? Five minutes? Ten? Sarah couldn't be sure. Then the man grabbed the girl. They struggled as he dragged her through a gap in the hedge at the top of the bank. Then there was nothing. Just the car and the bank and the road. And the sun.

There was no doubt at all who the man in the dream was. Even in the sometimes hazy and distorted perspective of the world of dreams the vision of the man now lying peacefully here beside her had been crystal clear.

David stirred, groaned and, without waking, rearranged his position in the bed. Sarah turned her head to look at him, his fine, softly curling locks giving him such a boyish, innocent air. Innocent? Oh God, what strange, disturbing tricks was her mind preparing to play on her now? She slid down further into the bed, clasped her hands behind her neck and stared at the ceiling. What was she looking for? She didn't know. But she knew there would be no more sleep. The dawn was already beginning to break, its half-light quietly, unceremoniously heralding the birth of a brand new day.

It was crazy, absolutely insane for her to set any store by a silly dream. It had just been her subconscious piecing together unrelated snippets from her waking consciousness. She was sure of it. And yet she knew that when David finally woke up, she wouldn't be able to tell him about it.

Sarah moved into David's apartment. When she thought about it afterwards, she couldn't remember which of them had suggested it. Nor did it matter. It had just seemed the most natural of developments. As natural as falling asleep when you were tired. She had been virtually living there anyway, and the final move had been more of a confirmation of that situation than a bold new decision. Yet it succeeded in bringing about a kind of wholesomeness to their relationship. Their lives became naturally more integrated and intimate.

They were with one another almost as much as before. But David, after cancelling all meetings and interviews for that first week with Sarah, now felt obliged to make himself more available to the people whom, after all, had been his original reason for coming to New York in the first place. So occasionally David would leave the apartment early for meetings with publishers, agents, film companies and anyone else in the process of making money out of the David Dent phenomenon. These meetings usually involved lunch as well. In fact, the business lunch in New York was, if anything, even more sacred than in London. But when this wasn't the case, at a prearranged time and place Sarah would meet him, and they would have lunch together.

It was on one of these occasions, after Sarah had been firmly ensconced in the Riverside Drive apartment for a week and a half, that they met in a pleasant little Italian restaurant just off Madison Avenue. David had just spent three or four hours discussing his new book with his editor and the Chief Executive at Smithson's, his American hardback publisher.

'I just don't know, Sarah,' he said, shaking his head, after they had ordered their food. 'I'm beginning to think that they're right. Perhaps it *is* madness for me to change my whole approach after only two books. Maybe I'm just not as firmly established as they all led me to believe. They seem to change the rules as it suits them. One minute they're telling me that I'm made. The world is my oyster. And the next they're saying "hold on a minute, you're not quite there yet". When I started off writing *The Defector*, it all seemed like an entertainment. After all, only one in a thousand writers makes any money. It was just a challenge. But everything seemed to get out of control. I was amazed when the agent called me telling me how much money I'd made before the book had even reached the streets. Let alone when the film deal came through. It all seemed like a fairy story.

'But writing *Chain Reaction* was a lot harder, and a lot less fun. I had a reputation to keep up, after only one book, and it hung round my neck like an albatross all the time I was writing it. I don't feel it's nearly as good as *The Defector*. But everyone else was enthusiastic, and the sales are just as good. I guess I've been really lucky. But when the film company offered to make *Chain Reaction*, I remembered just how much I'd disliked everything about the process with *The Defector*, and how I'd had no say at all in what happened to my book. This time, I've made sure that I get some kind of say in what goes on. And that's what's leading to all the trouble at the moment . . .'

The waitress brought David's spaghetti with clams and the fettucini Sarah had ordered.

'I've got to meet the people at World Pictures again to-morrow,' David continued. 'You'll never guess who they want for the lead in *Chain Reaction*. Gene Hackman. Can you believe it? Gene Hackman. Okay, sure he's good. Marvellous. But he's too old. The hero's only twenty-eight.' David sat facing her at the front of the restaurant, but with his back to the window. He hadn't been looking at Sarah as he spoke, but was concentrating on twirling the spaghetti around his fork. 'No, it's got to be someone younger,' he went on.

Sarah, who had also been keeping her eyes on her plate, looked up. Staring at her, impassively, inscrutably from the pavement on the other side of the window behind David was a face. *The* face. The face she had known as well as her own. Penny's face. The same one she had seen turn to her on the afternoon of that first meeting with David. The sudden shock of what she saw triggered a momentary nervous reaction and her hand involuntarily moved, and knocked her glass of red wine shattering to the floor. The waitress was there instantly, smiling, friendly and consoling. And in thirty seconds the mess was cleared and a new glass had been brought. But when Sarah had composed herself again and she looked at the window, the face had gone, as if it had never been.

'Are you all right?' David asked.

'Er, yes. I think so,' she answered uncertainly. 'I'm just so clumsy sometimes.' She gave a little smile that she knew probably didn't appear all that authentic. 'Now, what were you saying?'

'Well, the trouble is, everyone I suggest for the part is already spoken for for about a year ahead.' David's own preoccupations with the film company took the upper hand.

Sarah shivered. She was hardly listening to what David was saying. All she could think of was that face. Penny's face. What was happening? Was she going mad?

'Do you think I'm being silly?' David concluded.

Sarah looked into his eyes and consciously shook her wandering thoughts back into regular shape.

'No, I don't think you're being silly, at all. I think you're being absolutely wonderful, my love,' she said.

★ ★ ★

The next morning David left the apartment at nine-thirty. Sarah had been vaguely aware of his departure, as she felt him gently kiss her. But she hadn't really been sufficiently awake to respond. It was getting on for an hour later that she finally collected together the energy and the will to launch herself out of bed. She took a shower and mused on how much more powerful and refreshing the showers here were compared with those in England. Perhaps that was one of the reasons why Americans, particularly in New York, seemed so much more alert and active.

She washed her hair as well, and after a cursory going-over with a towel, she donned her bath-robe and went into the bedroom to give it a good brush-through. She was going to meet David at about one o'clock on Park Avenue, not far from Grand Central Station. If she walked, it would probably take about forty-five minutes. So she still had over an hour to kill.

Sarah sauntered into the kitchen, opened the door of the enormous, cavernous refrigerator and took out an open carton of orange juice. She poured herself a glassful and wandered absently with it into the sitting room. Then her eye was caught by something. A pale grey, cardboard folder lying on the table. She walked over to the table, casually picked up the folder and opened it. Tucked into the pocket were three sheets of paper, clipped together at the top left-hand corner. The top sheet was blank except for two lines of typed copy in the middle, which read: Storyline for *Call Back Yesterday* (working title) by David Dent.

Sarah closed the folder immediately, and placed it back on the table. If David didn't want anyone to see his new synopsis, whatever the reasons, sensible or silly, she would respect his wishes. After all, they must be able to trust one another. She walked over to the sofa and sat down, her eyes still fixed on the harmless-looking, yet increasingly mysterious grey folder.

But what David didn't know, wouldn't upset him, she thought. She would never tell another living soul. Never. It would be her secret. Her own secret. We're still individuals, with our own thoughts. Our own mysteries. If we knew absolutely everything about one another, there would be nothing left to explore. Anyway one of David's secrets from her was this very folder's contents. So why shouldn't one of hers be to know those contents? She got up, marched determinedly over to the table and sat down on one of the six chairs that surrounded it. Then she opened the folder and began to read . . .

It was just unbelievable. David's synopsis for *Call Back Yesterday* seemed to bear an incredible resemblance to what was happening to them now. You only had to change a few locations and circumstances and it could be their own story. But not only that. There were references to things in the past which came unsettlingly close to events she remembered only too well. Things concerning Penny about which David shouldn't, couldn't, have the slightest notion.

Sarah felt almost light-headed as she turned to the last page. But as she did so, she heard a jangling of keys from the hall outside the apartment. Her ears pricked up to the sound of a key being slotted into the lock. David. He must have come back for some reason. In an instant she had collected the sheets of paper together, put them into the folder and placed it more or less in its original position on the table. It was fortunate that two more locks had to be negotiated before entry to the apartment could be gained, because she had time to scoop up her empty glass and run into the kitchen.

'I'm back, Sarah.' David's voice boomed as he closed the door behind him.

Sarah stood in the doorway of the kitchen, as though she had been there all the time. She forced a smile of mild surprise and followed him into the sitting room.

'Was the meeting cancelled, or something?' she said.

'Well, not exactly.' David slumped onto the sofa. 'I sort of walked out I'm afraid. Well, they got me so mad. It's just impossible to reason with those people at World Pictures.'

Sarah noticed him glance momentarily at the table, and then look away immediately. He smiled appealingly at her. 'Hey, love. You couldn't get me some Coke out of the fridge, could you?'

Sarah, glad of any chance to compose herself, went back into the kitchen, over to the refrigerator and took out a large bottle of Coca Cola. But while she was pouring from it into a glass she could hear David moving about in the sitting room. The folder, she thought. She poured more orange juice for herself as well and carried both glasses from the kitchen. She handed him his and joined him on the sofa. The folder had disappeared from the table.

'So how did you leave it with them?' Sarah asked.

'Oh, I don't know really. And I certainly don't know why they bother to seek my opinions, if they're just going to ignore me. I wrote the damn book, after all. I created the characters. And I know how I see them.' David downed the Coke in one, and gave a long, satisfied sigh. 'Phew, I needed that. Now I'm just going to have a quick shower, and then we can go and have some lunch, as planned.'

David took his shower. But as she sat, vaguely aware of the distant sound of gushing water from the bathroom, Sarah's mind was confused and unsettled. What could it all mean? It was uncanny. Her imagination began to weave elaborate fantasies. Did David really leave the offending folder out by accident? And if he didn't – if it was all part of some mysterious game – then from what she'd read . . . No, it just wasn't possible, not at all conceivable. It had to be coincidence. None of it made sense. There were so many unanswered questions. For example, Penny's tragic death. Somehow, and God only knew how, it had made a strange, disconcerting and only slightly altered reappearance in David's synopsis too. And what about Penny? Were the recent apparitions only in Sarah's still slightly unbalanced mind? It all seemed so ridiculous. But she was sure there must be perfectly reasonable explanations. It would all sort itself out. And in the end she would wonder how she could have possibly harboured such crazy thoughts.

The next few days were uneasy ones for Sarah and David. David was particularly preoccupied with his contretemps with World Pictures. It seemed to make him sullen and withdrawn. Sarah tried her best to placate him. Perhaps a quiet, relaxed evening with Cathy and Frank would help. She talked it over with Cathy, and they agreed that she and David would go over to the Robsons' for dinner. But it didn't seem to have much effect on David's mood. In contrast to the invigorating conversations he and Cathy usually had on these occasions, David hardly said a word all evening. When he wasn't being actually morose, Sarah would catch sight of him staring distantly into space, his mind apparently on other things. She couldn't believe that it was just this silly film business doing it. There had to be more to it than that. But when she asked him about it, he just said:

'No, no. It's nothing really. It's just that the whole thing is getting me down a bit.'

. . . *Neil Benson is a well-known, young, fashion photographer, with psychopathic tendencies* . . .

Sarah wasn't fully convinced. David's new moodiness was reawakening the feelings of uneasiness that she had managed to push to the distant recesses of her mind. On several occasions, when Sarah was in the apartment alone, she hunted around trying to locate the grey folder. But to no avail. What was on the last page of David's synopsis? How did the book end? And was the same ending in store for them? Or was David's book following the events of their own story?

This is ridiculous, she said to herself. I'm just fantasizing. Things like that only happen in Hitchcock movies. I'm creating suspicion and doubt where they just don't exist.

David's mood seemed to change again. He suddenly became more accessible and more affectionate towards Sarah than he had been for nearly a week. The chief executive of Smithson's, David's American publishers, a man called Henry Bloom, was throwing a party at his home on Long Island to which David and partner were invited.

'Well, "partner". What do you say?' David asked in his best John Wayne voice.

'Well, I don't mind if I do,' Sarah replied in true Barbara Stanwyck style.

'It's going to be on Saturday night. It'll be great. Just about everyone who's anyone will be there. You never know, you could get spotted as the new Meryl Streep.' He paused and looked at her face carefully. 'Have I ever told you that you look a bit like her? Meryl Streep, I mean.'

'No, you haven't. You were a little late on that one, I'm afraid. Other people have mentioned it though. Black mark against you.'

'Well, you don't actually look like her double. A sort of younger, softer version, if you like.' He gave her a big hug. 'But I'll take Sarah Brownlow in preference, every time.'

'I should think so too.'

This was more like the old David. Warm and caring. And loving. That night they made love for the first time in over a week. So magical. Rapturous. It blossomed with new intensity, not just continuing where they had left off. But almost stepping into another gear. A sort of overdrive which transported them effortlessly onto a new plateau of shared ecstasy. And intimacy.

Everything was going to be fine.

FIVE

The Blooms' house was situated just outside Huntington village, on Long Island, about forty miles from the centre of Manhattan. David had hired a car for the weekend, and as they drove slowly through the village Sarah thought the whole place had a vaguely English air about it.

'Walt Whitman, the poet, used to live here, you know,' said David.

'When was that?' said Sarah.

'Oh, I don't know exactly. He died sometime in the 1880s. And I think he may have spent his last years here. But I wouldn't swear to it. Ah, I think this is it.'

They turned into the driveway and followed its sweeping curve up to the house.

'My God, look at that place,' Sarah gasped.

The house sprawled elegantly before them, its white New England style exterior sparkling from the reflected spotlights placed strategically in the grounds. The interior was even more spectacular – spacious and open, with huge, sweeping staircases going off in all directions. And it was packed with people, drinking, talking and laughing. Mrs Bloom greeted them at the front door.

'It's David, isn't it? David Dent.' She smiled a distant, polite smile. 'I'm Marion Bloom.' She turned to Sarah. 'And you are . . . ?'

'Oh, I'm sorry. Please forgive me.' He put his hand on Sarah's shoulder and grinned proudly. 'This is Sarah Brownlow.'

Marion Bloom was a short, petite, attractive woman in her early fifties. What had once been a fine Brooklyn nose had had the steam taken out of it by surgery, leaving one that was straighter and shorter, if a little less interesting. Her too perfectly shaped teeth gleamed with an unreal exuberance as she smiled.

'I'm very pleased you could come, Sarah. Now please, both of you, go and get yourselves a drink and some food.' She pointed towards the back of the house. 'It's all being served from the patio outside.'

Sarah and David made their way past the numerous clutches of people, some of whom were engaged in loud, animated conversation, punctuated by whoops of laughter, while others muttered quietly to one another as though organizing some secret deal.

Sarah noticed a suit-clad John Updike closeted in conversation with the greying and more casually dressed Norman Mailer. Mailer seemed to be doing most of the talking, with Updike contributing a sympathetic ear and the odd comment of his own. Waiters circulated, weaving in and out of the groups of guests carrying trays of exotic-looking cocktails. The inside of the Blooms' house really was beautiful. A plush, stone-grey carpet seemed to cover every single inch of floor area and the elegant Regency furniture was only one example of the Blooms' superb collection of antiques. The glass cabinet full of capo di monte pieces must be worth a fortune, Sarah thought. And that looked suspiciously like an original Constable landscape hanging proudly over the elaborately carved fireplace.

'How many face-lifts do you think she's had?' Sarah said quietly out of the corner of her mouth.

'Who?'

'Mrs Bloom.'

'Oh, about seventeen, I should think,' was David's deadpan reply.

Sarah giggled as they found themselves on the patio faced by a daunting row of tables draped in crisp white tablecloths, and displaying a remarkable array of hot and cold food.

'Huh, some spread,' said David. 'I'm starving.'

Sarah had taken the opportunity to dress up for the occasion. It was the first time that such a chance had really arisen. Most of the time so far she had spent wearing jeans and T-shirts or loose, flowing casual dresses that didn't cling to her too much in the heat. But tonight, with her long, rich blonde hair raised elegantly to a bun, and wearing a pink, mid-length Yves St Laurent dress, she looked stunning. David's jaw had dropped in amazement as she had come out of the bedroom before they left the apartment, the transformation complete.

'My God. Aphrodite had better watch out. You look incredible. I can see I'm going to have my work cut out keeping hold of you this evening. You'll probably be whisked off by some Hollywood film producer. And I'll never see you again,' he said.

Sarah had put her arms around his neck, kissed his lips and rubbed her nose gently against his.

'Don't worry. I'll write to you sometimes. I may even send for you to accompany me to my Oscar presentation,' she had teased. David had smacked her playfully on the bottom.

The night was perfect. Warm and caressing, and without the discomfort and stickiness they'd had to endure in the city recently. Sarah pieced together a modest salad for herself from the selection before them. With two full meals a day, and a little less walking in the last week or so, she was beginning to feel her clothes closing in around her bottom and thighs. David piled his plate with a sample of every meat he could find. Beef, turkey, chicken, pastrami, tongue and more – then smothered them with creamy potato and Russian salads and coleslaw. Sarah had never known anyone with an appetite anywhere near the size of David's, yet he never seemed to put on any weight. Or none that Sarah had noticed. She supposed that all the calories were used up by David's indefatigable nervous energy. Or else his metabolism must be different to hers.

'David. Hi. Glad you could make it.' Sarah and David both turned to find a beaming, middle-aged man bearing down on them. He smiled broadly at Sarah. 'And this, presumably, is Sarah.'

'Yes. Sarah Brownlow, Henry Bloom, chief executive at Smithson's. The man who's giving me a hard time at the moment,' joked David.

Bloom drew contentedly on his enormous cigar and exhaled a billowing cloud of smoke into the air above their heads.

'Aw, come on. This is a party. No business. Well not that kind of business, anyway. If someone from Bantam or Avon happens to mention, over their martini, that they're interested in paying a million bucks' advance for your new book,' Bloom raised his hands and shrugged, 'then that sort of business we can handle.'

Henry Bloom was now fifty-six. Short and stocky with a waistline abused by too many business lunches, he was nevertheless an attractive man. His full head of curly, greying, hair, and his sparkling, busy eyes gave him an almost boyish quality which Sarah found quite appealing. But his most outstanding feature was something which a man in his position needed above everything else. Henry Bloom had personality. It oozed out of him with effortless panache. He could cajole, plead or, if it were necessary, be firm with such style and charm, that one was almost hypnotized into accepting whatever he wanted them to.

Bloom's rise to one of the top jobs in American publishing had become a legend of fairy-tale proportions. He had worked his way up, in forty years, from the post of messenger boy in the mailroom to one of the top jobs in American publishing, chief executive at Smithson's, a post he had held for nine years. And in those nine years Bloom had grown in stature and confidence to such an extent that he now gave the impression of being bigger than the job. He had brought Smithson's to new peaks of commercial success, making the David Dents of this world household names with only one or two books to their credit. The big deals – selling the paperback and film rights of books – he insisted on conducting himself. And he very rarely failed. He had made it his business in the last nine years to get to know the biggest people in the world of entertainment. Whether it be a top Hollywood actor, or an influential T.V. producer, Bloom would woo them with his consummate charm, and they would be in his pocket for whenever he needed to make use of them.

And quite a selection of those pocketed personalities were whooping it up at the Blooms' this very evening.

Sarah was really enjoying herself. This was certainly the life to lead. And she had a unique chance to view it all as an outsider, who wasn't really part of it. Then she would consciously concentrate her thoughts, and drift back into the realization that it *was* all real. That it was all actually happening.

Bloom prepared to politely extricate himself from their little group, in order to mix with his other guests. But before he left them, he moved into a position between them and placed his arms around their respective shoulders.

'Now before you two leave this evening, I want to talk to you again.' Bloom lowered his voice, as though he were about to confide to them some long held secret. 'I have a little proposition for you that I think you'll find pretty enticing.' He winked at them. 'See you later.' And he was gone.

They had been at the party for two or three hours drifting from group to group. Sarah had quite lost track of the time. David was really shining in these surroundings with his easy, unselfconscious charm. Yet, when she thought about it, he was being no different to when they were alone. But, she supposed, that was the thing that *was* so impressive. The fact that in this, what she found to be quite awe-inspiring situation, there was nothing pretentious in David's behaviour, whatsoever.

Now they had found a quiet little corner, and were chatting intimately between themselves about some of the people they had spoken to and about how they should, perhaps, soon think about beginning the hour's drive back into the city.

'Hello, there.'

Sarah looked up quickly, before she had even consciously realized that the voice which had uttered the words was actually familiar to her. It was Andrew Simpson. The same Andrew Simpson she had been so rude to at Kennedy Airport the day she had arrived. 'I think I must have walked past you half a dozen times this evening without recognizing you. You look so different.'

Sarah was somewhat flummoxed and embarrassed. She had forgotten all about Andrew Simpson. What could she possibly say to this man from whom she had stormed away, without even saying goodbye? But she thought it was probably best, now she was in this awkward position, to begin with some kind of apology.

'Look. I really am terribly sorry about my behaviour that day. I just don't know what came over me,' she said. 'Oh, by the way, this is David Dent, a friend of mine. David, this is Andrew Simpson. We met on the flight coming over from England. And I'm afraid I was very rude to him.' Sarah assumed a contrite expression.

The two men nodded to one another. Then Simpson, with that effortless, charming smile she now remembered so well, turned to Sarah.

'Please don't apologize. You were probably very tired after the flight and, well, you may have slightly misunderstood my er . . . intentions. I quite understand.'

There was an uncomfortable pause before Simpson spoke again. 'So what is your connection with the inimitable Mr Bloom?'

From then on the conversation between Sarah and Simpson became much easier, as though some barrier had been broken. But David didn't look as though he had taken to Simpson. He replied to the man's questions only in clipped monosyllables, and appeared not to have the slightest intention of expanding their conversation.

Simpson's own relationship with the Blooms was also a business one. But in a different way.

'If you look around this whole house,' he said, 'most of the antiques you'll see, Henry bought from or through me. You see, I know his taste exactly. Whenever I get hold of something I think he'll like, I'll bring it down to New York to show him specially. And if there's something he particularly wants, then I'll try and get it for him.'

They continued chatting, but Sarah just occasionally caught the odd glimpse of Simpson looking at her. Staring really. And she could only describe his expression as one of concerned confusion. But whenever he became aware that Sarah had noticed this, his face instantly softened and dissolved into its more familiar facade of friendliness and charm.

They talked some more about New York. Sarah gave a long spiel about what they had done and seen so far, and what they were planning to do in the near future. But David's rudeness and sullenness was beginning to irritate Sarah a little. And as friendly and pleasant Simpson continued to be towards David, he would still come back at him with the odd short, sour comment. She waited for a slight pause in the conversation and then said:

'Well, if you'll excuse us, Andrew, we've got a longish drive back to Manhattan.' She glanced at David, but he didn't seem to have heard what she said. His slight frown suggested that his mind was definitely on other things.

'Oh, right. Of course. I shall be staying here, myself. The Blooms' breakfasts are so good. Almost as good as in England,' he said. 'Different, of course. But good.' Simpson paused as though there was something else he wanted to say, but he didn't quite know how to phrase it. Eventually,

55

he seemed to have decided on the right words. 'By the way, that invitation is still open, you know. Either for yourself, Sarah, or both of you. There's plenty of room.'

Sarah smiled, appreciatively. And genuinely. She had really quite warmed to Simpson again during their talk. Perhaps she *had* misunderstood his intentions when they first met. The flight had probably made her more tired than she thought. And David was rather annoying her with his obvious discourtesy.

'That's very kind of you, Andrew. Especially as I so rudely responded to your first invitation. I think I must still have the address in my bag somewhere.'

'Well, in case you haven't . . .' And Simpson proceeded to jot down all the details again for her. They said their goodbyes, although David's was little more than a mutter, and Simpson moved off, leaving Sarah and David alone. There was a frosty silence between them for a moment. But Sarah was determined to have it out with him.

'Just tell me why you were so rude to him,' she said.

David was silent. He bit his lip nervously.

'There was just something about him I didn't like,' he replied eventually. 'I don't know what it was. I can't put my finger on it.'

'Well, that's as maybe.' There was a sharpness to Sarah's voice. 'But you could have had the decency to be civil. Even if it was just for my sake.'

David sighed.

'I'm sorry, love. I suppose you're right. It's just that he sort of gave me the creeps. He was too smooth. Too knowing. Too much in control. It just didn't ring true. No real reason at all. But I just wouldn't trust him.'

Sarah felt bound to confess to herself that she actually thought David was wrong, and wondered if there might be just the slightest element of jealousy colouring his opinion.

'He's quite attractive, I must say,' she reflected.

'If you like that sort of thing, I suppose. Middle-aged, sophisticated and good-looking. And well aware of it. You can see it a mile off. I don't know how women get taken in so easily by men like that.'

'Perhaps they want to. Have you never thought of that?'

David looked thoughtful for a moment.

'Yes, I suppose they do.' He paused for a second. 'Do you know what. I think one day I'll write a romance under a pseudonym. Like one of those Mills and Boon things. All exotic locations, perfect summer days and endless love. Oh, and a happy ending.'

David went off to try and find the Blooms while Sarah made her way past the thinning clutches of people to the main staircase, thinking a trip to the bathroom would be a sensible idea before the drive home. She had climbed halfway up when she turned to view the proceedings from this revealing vantage point. The effect was one of detaching her again from the chatter and the laughter below. She was observing it all as though from the outside, and, for a brief moment, it all struck her as a little silly. All those 'plastic', superficial people pretending to be nice to one another. She sighed. No, that wasn't fair. It was just that David's reaction to Andrew Simpson had left a bad taste in her mouth. Made her feel a bit sour. She gazed around some more and suddenly her attention was caught by a young woman. Sarah couldn't get a proper view of her. Only her back, much of which was laid bare by a scanty bright blue dress, and a little bit of her face. She was standing alone, sipping what looked to be champagne from an elegant, thin-stemmed goblet. Sarah strained to try and get a better look, nearly losing her footing on the stairs in the process. It just couldn't be. But the hair was identical, as was the slim but shapely figure. *Penny.*

Sarah began to perspire and shiver at the same time. For a moment she was rooted to the spot. Trapped and paralysed by fear. Shock. The girl began to move away. Sarah raced down the sweeping staircase to follow her, knocking a glass clean out of someone's hand as she reached the bottom. She stopped and apologized to the sun-tanned middle-aged woman who had lost what remained of her martini. Sarah moved on in the direction which the girl had followed, right through to the patio at the back. But there was absolutely no sign of her. What could have happened to her? Was she beginning to lose her senses? Perspiring and a little breathless she walked slowly back to the stairs. She felt weak, almost drained. She climbed heavily to the top and went into the bathroom. The cold water on her face was refreshing and sobering. That's what it must be, she thought. She had drunk too much. She was imagining things that just weren't there. . .

Shakily, she rejoined David, who had been waylaid by the Blooms' daughter, Rachel. She was an unattractive girl with long, unwieldy black hair who had unfortunately inherited two rather uncomplimentary qualities from her parents: a certain portliness and the lack of height required to make it less obvious. But she was friendly, energetic and enthusiastic. And, like her father, a tremendously entertaining conversationalist.

'Oh, there you are.' Henry Bloom's voice bellowed above the general party hubbub which was beginning to diminish a little now, as some of the guests were starting to leave and make their way home. 'I've been looking for you.'

David thanked Bloom, on behalf of Sarah and himself, for a super evening. Sarah reiterated her own gratitude.

'Yes, it's been absolutely wonderful. And your house is just a dream.'

'I'm just glad David decided to let us all have a look at you. He's been keeping you under wraps, a bit, hasn't he?'

Sarah thought about it. It was true, she hadn't met any of the people David had originally come to New York to see – publishers, agents and the like. She had never considered it strange before. After all, as far as she knew, at least in the time she had known David, he hadn't mixed socially with those people anyway. But there had been something in the way Henry Bloom had spoken which made it all sound slightly menacing and mysterious. And when she looked at David, yes, he was smiling. But a little uncomfortably, she suspected. It was undoubtedly her good old imagination again. Making mountains out of non-existent molehills. Still, David wasn't really in her good books at the moment.

'Remember what I said about having a proposition to make you,' said Bloom. 'Well, Smithson's have an apartment down in the Hamptons. Couple of bedrooms, all mod cons. Hot and cold running water etcetera,' he joked. 'Lots of companies have them all over the place. We've got another one in Florida, and a house on the West Coast, just outside Los Angeles. The thing is, the Hamptons apartment is free for a couple of weeks. And I'd kind of like for you two to stay there if you wanted. I think it would be good for you to get out of New York for a little while. Come August, it'll probably get even more humid in the city.' Bloom looked serious for a moment, and put his hand on David's shoulder. 'And, to be honest, David, I think you need some time to think about things.'

David and Sarah glanced at each other and the meeting of their eyes confirmed that they were both of the opinion that it would be a great thing to do.

'Sounds fine, Henry. Thank you,' David said. 'I'll call you in the next couple of days to sort out the details.'

SIX

Sarah propped herself up by her two elbows and looked out towards the sea from her position on the beach. Who was it who wrote about the 'wine dark sea' she thought? She racked her brains for a moment. She was sure it was someone Greek. Homer or someone like that. Whoever it was, those few words really evoked the deep richness of the sea she saw now, stretching out in its spacious freedom to meet the perfect clear blue sky at the horizon.

East Hampton really was a beautiful place. Relatively unspoilt, it hadn't yet succumbed to the seediness and commercialism of Coney Island. She had been desperately disappointed in the place when she and David had taken the ferry to that legendary spot. East Hampton was the sophisticated summer playground of New York's young and chic. Groups of kids from affluent middle-class families would rent houses for the summer, and take turns at staying in them; while the really wealthy had their own houses and apartments there as summer retreats.

'The whole place just reeks of comfort and affluence,' David had said.

'Well, I'm not complaining. Are you?' Sarah had replied.

They had been at East Hampton for a couple of days now. The apartment owned by Smithson's was, as they had expected, the height of luxury. It was spacious and elegantly appointed, with modern Scandinavian-styled furniture in brilliant whites, bright reds and blues. And when the sun flooded in through the large windows and kissed everything in its path with its dazzling beam, it all reminded Sarah of something out of the Sunday colour supplements at home, or a Habitat catalogue. Everything was there ready for them. A refrigerator full of food, and a drinks cabinet stuffed so full that it nearly all fell out when David first opened it.

On the previous evening they had made themselves dinner from the contents of the bulging refrigerator. Poached salmon was one of David's favourite dishes, and he was excited at the prospect of eating it for the first time since he had left England. And as they had sat in the candlelight listening to the sea's waves, not a hundred yards away, gently breaking and then caressing the sand with their lush white foam, Sarah mused to herself on how this was possibly the most perfect, most idyllic night of her life.

But it wasn't merely the romantic sounds and setting which made it all seem so wonderful. In a sense they were the icing on the cake. The frills and decorations around the nucleus of her euphoria. David. She could go on listening to him talk for hours, his voice soft and full, his conversation a perfect synthesis of heart-felt seriousness and amusing notions and anecdotes. And much more than any man she had known, David was teaching her things. Not just tangibles, Gradgrind's 'facts' if you like, but something about how to absorb them and use them. And yet he wasn't doing this consciously, patronizingly. He was just being David Dent. He was almost boyish in his unselfconsciousness, becoming wholly consumed in whatever he was talking or joking about. Sarah found it all quite exhilarating. She was thrilled by his intellectual agility, sent into uncontrollable spasms of laughter by his clowning, and truly touched by his unpretentiousness. And she found him very sexy, too. It all added up to a wholesomeness, a completeness, which somehow made David seem very real. And sometimes she would see in his eyes, as she had on that evening, a look which called to her to become part of that completeness. And she would simply melt away with the sheer joy of it.

That night they had made love to the timeless, perpetual rhythm of the sea, and Sarah, lost in the enveloping rapture of the moment, knew that if it were possible to experience paradise on earth, then this unquestionably was it.

And now, as she lay on the softly undulating curves of the sand, she still glowed with the embers of last night's passionate fire. She squinted into the bright sun, whose dazzling reflection danced on the sea's surface. She was looking for David, who had left her ten or fifteen minutes before to go for a swim. She thought she caught sight of him. He was quite a long way out, though so was the tide, and the water only seemed to come up to his chest. But there was also someone else. Someone standing very close to him. It was a woman. A youngish woman with blonde, shoulder-length hair. Sarah tried to shield her eyes from the sun, and cursed herself for leaving her sunglasses back at the apartment. *Penny*. Sarah sat up with a start. She gave a big gulp, but her throat had gone dry. She was breathing quite quickly, now. The young woman was certainly looking at David. She might even be talking to him. But he didn't seem to be taking much notice of her as he now floated on his back.

At that moment a group of six or seven kids in their late teens walked past Sarah and, for a few seconds, obscured her view. But when they had gone, something very strange had happened. The woman in the sea had disappeared. David was still there, floating not only physically, but mentally too, she imagined. Alone with the sun and the sea, and his thoughts. For he was certainly alone now. There seemed to be no sign of the girl at all. Sarah's eyes scoured as much of the sea as was in her view. There weren't many people in the water, so it was unlikely that she could have lost sight of her in a mass of sea-bathers. She lay down again and closed her eyes. Was it the sun, this time, playing tricks on her? How much longer was she going to be able to go on finding excuses for these visions? If they *were* visions. No, more likely they were just coincidences that her mind was contriving to seem more sinister than was the case.

She must have dozed off, because the next thing she was

aware of was the sudden sensation of cold sea water droplets on her sun-oil-soaked stomach. She sat up with a jolt to find David deliberately shaking his wet hair over her.

'David. You frightened the life out of me,' she said.

'Sorry, love. But I just couldn't resist it. You looked so decadent and smug lying there. I thought you needed a bit of a shock to bring you back to earth.' He chuckled aloud, though really to himself. 'That's what life is all about, you know. Ups and downs. Dozy contentment punctuated by sudden shocks of joy or sorrow, ecstasy or pain.'

'You're being very profound, all of a sudden,' Sarah said, leaning on one elbow and watching David dry himself. He does have rather a nice body, she thought, as she studied him appreciatively. Slim, but well-proportioned. 'So that's what you've been doing out there. Working out the mysteries of life?' She paused slightly. 'As well as chatting up strange women.'

David looked up with a mildly puzzled expression.

'Sorry?' he said.

'Come on, Casanova.' Sarah laughed. 'Own up. I've caught you red-handed.'

David, who had now finished drying himself, stood astride Sarah, crossed his arms and looked down at her with mock disapproval.

'Now what, may I ask, is this all about?' he said.

'That girl in the sea who seemed so interested in you. You looked as if you were being very cool, I must say. Perhaps that's what frightened her away in the end.'

David seemed even more puzzled now. He sat down beside her.

'What girl? There wasn't anyone within fifty yards of me, as far as I was aware.'

Sarah felt a wave of doubt pass through her.

'But I saw her,' she said.

'Are you sure you didn't dream it while you were dozing?' David ventured.

'No, of course I didn't,' Sarah snapped irritably. She lay her head down again, and used her forearm to cover her eyes from the sun. And then, feeling a pang of remorse for her sudden flash of anger, she reached out for David's arm with her other hand.

'I'm sorry, love,' she said. 'I didn't mean to snap. It must be the sun.' She paused. 'Or something.'

David leaned across and kissed her delicately on the forehead.

'That's okay. Don't worry, darling,' he said softly. 'I think it must be lack of food. Let's go and have some lunch.'

'Yes.'

They had decided to make full use of Henry Bloom's kind offer, and stay at the apartment for the whole two weeks of its availability. Hiring a car while in Manhattan was unnecessary and more trouble than it was worth. Taxis were plentiful when somewhere was too far away to walk. And parking was simply a nightmare anyway. But out on Long Island it was the complete opposite. A car was an absolute necessity. So David hired a brand new bright blue Chevrolet Impala, similar to the one owned by the Robsons, who paid a fortune for garaging theirs in the city. When they weren't sun-bathing, swimming or strolling around, stopping off at sun-drenched sidewalk cafés for ice-cold Budweisers, they would drive out to explore the island.

Long Island seemed to Sarah almost too good to be true. It was just so comfortable, so confident and sure of itself. It was partly the place. But it was also the people. Everyone there seemed to enjoy such a good life. There they were, out of the pollution and noise of the city, and yet within easy reach of it, either for working or for dipping, at their leisure, into its non-stop, effervescent night-life. And because everyone seemed to have a car the whole island seemed a lot smaller than it actually was. People drove everywhere. A twenty-mile car ride to one of the many shopping malls that peppered the island was, for them, the equivalent to popping down the road to the local shops back in England. So much space. And yet for Long Islanders there was nothing daunting about it. They relished it. They were used to it. And now, of course, they needed it. Sarah supposed that this was what characterized Americans in general, although she hated generalizations. They were an expansive people. Not so much physically large, but big in outlook and expectations. And Sarah thought that it must emanate originally from being surrounded by all that space. All those natural resources and opportunities.

They sat outside what had become their favourite café overlooking the beach. David was reading a tatty old paperback. It was D. H. Lawrence's *Sons and Lovers*, one of his favourite novels. The shabby, yellowing edition he held delicately in his hands to prevent any more pages from falling out, was now on its fourth outing. Sarah had just been sitting there, sipping at her beer, watching the lazy East Hampton afternoon gently pass on its way towards what was undoubtedly going to be another beautiful evening. She wore her hair up in a red and white polka-dotted head scarf. This enabled her to keep her blonde locks, bleached even fairer by the sun, from smothering her neck and shoulders. A welcome relief in ninety degrees of heat. It also protected her head from direct contact with the sun's powerful rays, which had recently begun to cause her headaches. She also wore a white, short-sleeved shirt, with its lower half tied around the bottom of her rib-cage, revealing her smooth, golden-tanned midriff, and a pair of brief shorts cut down from an old faded pair of jeans.

'Do you know what?' she said. It was the first time either of them had spoken for about fifteen minutes. David looked up from his book.

'What's that?' he asked.

'I think I could live here. Perhaps not here in East Hampton. It's almost too perfect. Sort of unreal. But on Long Island, a bit closer to the city. Say where the Blooms live. That sort of area.' She sighed. 'They've got the best of both worlds there. The clean air and the lovely big houses. And just a short drive away from probably the most exciting city in the world.'

'But you can get that in England as well,' David said as he placed his book face down on the table. 'And you don't have to drive out so far from the city to get to the countryside.'

Sarah looked pensive for a moment.

'Yes, I suppose you're right. But it doesn't seem to have the spaciousness of this place.'

'Mm, I can see what you mean,' David said, as he glanced towards the beach at the bronzed American kids splashing in the sea and tossing their frisbees high into the cloudless, deep blue sky. Sarah placed her elbows on the table and leaned forward, resting her chin on her cupped hands.

'David, we haven't discussed anything about the future, you know.'

'Which future do you mean? Short term or long term?' he replied.

'Well, both really, I suppose. But more specifically, the next couple of months. You haven't said how long you're going to stay in New York.'

'Do I have to?' David smiled. 'Isn't it obvious?' He also leaned forward, towards her, took both her hands from her face, and held one in each of his own. 'I want to stay here for as long as you're here.' He kissed the palm of her left hand, and she felt a tingling sensation of pleasure shoot through her. How stupid she was to have had those crazy thoughts about David. All that nonsense about his silly storyline for *Call Back Yesterday*. Just pure coincidence made to look sinister by her vivid imagination. And that reminded her. 'What about your new novel? What are you going to do about it?'

David stiffened visibly and looked uncomfortable, but only just long enough for Sarah to be aware of it. In an instant he had relaxed again. 'I think I'm going to go ahead with it as it is,' he said.

'But will they publish it?' Sarah asked.

'I don't know. But I do know that I've got to have the courage of my convictions. I think it'll work. And I believe it can be as commercial as anything else I've done.'

Sarah watched him carefully. That moment of uncertainty and discomfort in David's manner as she had suddenly, without warning, brought the subject up, was worrying her again. She decided that now was the time to press him further.

'David, do you trust me?' she whispered.

'Why yes. Of course I do.' His reply was accompanied by a puzzled furrowing of his brow. 'Why do you ask?'

'Well, it's your new book.' She paused with a sigh, and searched for the right words and approach with which to tackle him on the subject. 'It's just that I feel it's a big barrier between us. It's a very important thing in your life at the moment. It's obviously taking up a lot of your thoughts. And . . . well, it's a whole chunk of you that I don't know anything about.' She winced inwardly at this little lie and the twinge of guilt she felt. Here she was trying to persuade David to confide in her, and yet she hadn't been totally straight with him. But if he told her about it, the whole thing, then that would release Sarah from her guilt because what she already knew about the story, she would be entitled to know anyway. She continued. 'I may be able to help in some way. Make suggestions. Perhaps you need someone else who doesn't have a vested interest to give you an unbiased opinion.'

Sarah hadn't been looking at David as she was talking. She found it easier to collect her thoughts and words together if she didn't have her eyes on him. But now she looked up. David was staring at her with steady, slightly narrowed eyes, his face totally expressionless. It frightened her, made her shiver. She had never seen him look so cold before. So devoid of emotion. She was transfixed, almost hypnotized by his stare. And then he said:

'No, Sarah. I have to do it myself.' Then he got up from the table and walked away, in the direction of the apartment.

. . . It begins with a chance meeting on a deserted country road. A young girl stops on her bicycle by a man sitting in his car, which has broken down . . .

Sarah sat there for several minutes, her mind a confused blur. All the worries and doubts, and uncertainties returned. Suddenly she felt so distant from him. What she had just seen was a David she didn't really know. Didn't want to know. And yet the other David, the one who had been so diffident when they had met outside Macy's; who joked and laughed with her; who made love to her as though it were the last day of their lives. That was the David she loved with each and every part of her body and soul. But Sarah just couldn't get out of her mind the reality of David's synopsis. Of all the weird thoughts whirling around her mind at this time, most could be dismissed as distorted figments of imagination. But the outline for David's novel was something tangible. She had held it in her own hands, read it with her own eyes. The coincidence between its contents and these sightings of her dead sister seemed too great for her to ignore, especially when David reacted as he had just done. Was Penny trying to warn her? Oh, how she wished it would all become normal again. She was in love. Why should she have such sinister notions occupying her thoughts?

Perhaps she was over-reacting. Perhaps he was just angry that she seemed not to appreciate and respect his wishes concerning this one aspect of his life. Well, if that was the case, she had never seen him show his anger in quite that way before. She decided she'd let him cool off for a bit. So she called the waiter and ordered another beer. It was funny. She never drank beer back in England. She didn't really like the stuff. But she had quite taken to American beer. It seemed to have much more flavour than its English counterpart. The waiter brought her another Budweiser, which she poured and sipped slowly. She felt more relaxed now. The tension had loosened. She looked at her watch. It was ten past five, and the clearly defined shadows around her were beginning to slant and lengthen.

When Sarah got back to the apartment David was nowhere to be found. Perhaps he hadn't come back here after all, she thought. He must have gone for a stroll. She walked into the bedroom and flopped down onto the bed. The sun made her so tired. Even if she wasn't doing anything particularly strenuous, and she certainly hadn't been during their stay here in East Hampton, it seemed to drain her of all her energy. She heard the front door open.

'David?' she called.

'Yes, where are you?'

'In the bedroom.'

David appeared in the bedroom doorway holding an ice-cream cornet with two enormous scoops perched precariously on top of it. He had a wide grin on his face.

'Your moody man has returned,' he said as his expression changed to one of open contrition. And he shuffled comically over to the bed where he sat down beside Sarah. 'Would you like me to apologize? Or would you rather hit me?'

Sarah laughed. And as David went to take a bite from his ice-cream, she jogged his hand so that his nose ended up buried in the cornet. It started her giggling, and she just couldn't stop. David gave a resigned nod or two, and attempted to clear the ice-cream from his face. Sarah was laughing so much that it was beginning to hurt. It was funny. Yes, it was very funny. But her laughter wasn't pure mirth. There was something nervous there as well. That thin, almost indefinable line between comedy and pathos was, at that moment, barely perceptible. And Sarah's laughter was expressing both simultaneously.

Yes they had made up, on the face of it, in the way that lovers do. But it was something of an uneasy peace. Certainly uneasy for Sarah. There had been something cosmetic about it to her. Something which suggested that it had not reached as deeply as was apparent. The cracks had been covered up. But was the structure sound?

SEVEN

The Smithson offices were situated on the bottom four floors of one of the older office blocks on Madison Avenue. In old Charles Smithson's day they had been rather austere and stark. Even, it was whispered in publishing circles, cheap. Charles Smithson was off-beat and unconventional, to say the least. But he was also spartan in his ways and not a little mean. Whether the latter was a result of the former, or vice versa, people were never quite sure. But whatever the true facts about Charles Smithson's personality, the offices over which he presided certainly couldn't be mistaken for being plush. The parquet floors were mostly bare; paint peeled from the walls and ceiling; the lighting was abysmal; the heating in winter was minimal enough to seem non-existent; and there was no air-conditioning in summer.

When the old man died in 1974, and Henry Bloom was unanimously elected as chief executive, there were changes. The first thing Bloom did was to make sure the whole place got a new coat of paint. Then he had air-conditioning fitted and the ancient central heating system replaced. Gradually, over the next five years, the offices were transformed. Luxurious leather armchairs and sofas welcomed people to the reception area. A light grey, deep pile carpet almost squelched beneath the feet as one strolled from one office to another. And the office furniture dazzled with its brilliant white wood. But the *pièce de résistance* was the boardroom. It was a very large, tall room. An enormous, oval-shaped, plate-glass table-top supported by a gleaming tubular steel frame, stood imposingly in the middle of it. It was surrounded by a dozen high-backed, black leather chairs utilizing the same tubular design for their legs and arms. Tall, rich-green yucca and umbrella palm plants stood, sentry-like on the floor, around the perimeter. And a huge sparkling chandelier that resembled something out of *Star Wars*, hung dauntingly from the ceiling.

It was this sight which greeted Sarah and David, a few days after they had returned from East Hampton. David had telephoned Bloom to thank him for the use of the apartment and the two weeks of sun-soaked laziness that went with it. Bloom had mentioned the fact that he was having a small, informal gathering at the Smithson offices around cocktail time one evening during the following week, and insisted that David and Sarah should come along.

At one end of the room, behind two white-clothed tables displaying a varied selection of bottles and glasses, stood a barman in a starched, creaseless, white jacket, and sporting a black bow-tie. He was dispensing whisky sours, martinis and the like to the thirty or so people that milled around the huge room. Most of those present were top employees of Smithson's. But some of the other guests included literary agents and the odd Smithson's author. One of the latter was a bubbling, talkative woman in her mid-thirties who had made a substantial amount of money, both for herself and Smithson's, from a series of revolutionary new diet books. When Cindy Horowitz was in the vicinity, everyone knew it. Tall and slim, as befitted someone who claimed to have invented the perfect diet technique, she had one of those faces which, although it might not be considered pretty, could, and nevertheless was, regarded as attractive. Her finely etched cheekbones, clear, wide ice-blue eyes and her fiery shock of curly red hair made heads turn wherever she went. And with the addition of her ebullient personality, she was obviously a very promotable property indeed. She couldn't help but be the centre of attention, and in the Smithson's boardroom on this sticky August evening, she was certainly that. And, much to Sarah's annoyance, she had taken a rather obvious shine to David.

Henry Bloom took care of Sarah, while David seemed

imprisoned by the non-stop chatter and effervescence of Cindy Horowitz. Bloom introduced her to many of the people from Smithson's who were present, and whom David had met anyway on previous visits to New York. This made her feel considerably less aggrieved about Cindy Horowitz's apparent monopoly of David's attention. Henry Bloom was really taking very good care of her. She found it quite flattering, and something of a consolation when she looked over occasionally in David's direction where Cindy Horowitz was talking nineteen to the dozen and flashing those enormous, entrancing eyes. Yet the thing that irritated her most about the Cindy Horowitz invasion was the fact that she *did* get so annoyed. It would never have meant a thing to her two or three weeks before. She thought she trusted David. She was sure she had done. And now it seemed, almost without realizing it, that things had changed in a subtle, virtually imperceptible way. The consummate trust, the trust that existed without having to think about it, just didn't appear to be there any more. Ever since that cold, frightening stare David had given her outside the café in East Hampton she wasn't one hundred per cent at ease about the whole thing.

Although they had made up after their argument at the café, and seemed as friendly and as close as before, Sarah couldn't help feeling that a distance had emerged between them. A distance that she was perhaps evolving in her own mind as a defence mechanism against a truth which seemed too awful to contemplate. The visions of Penny had been shocking and unsettling on their own. But together with the uncanny coincidence of David's synopsis for *Call Back Yesterday*, they seemed to suggest an explanation that was unthinkable. She felt uneasy and unsure of everything. Insecure, she supposed. But as she looked across at David, trussed up in conversation with the Horowitz woman, observed his sensual smile, the soft, fine hair and those bright, fathomless eyes which often held her transfixed, she wondered whether that annoying pang of jealousy could be put down to one thing only. She was simply in love with him. If only it were that easy.

'Ah, look who's just come in,' said Bloom, who had hardly moved from Sarah's side since she and David had arrived.

In the doorway stood a middle-aged man. Slim and of average height, he had straight blond hair, parted on the left, a strong, angular jaw and a long, thin, pointed nose. But it was probably his dress that was most striking. He looked as though he had just come off a cricket field. He wore a white, open-necked shirt, white flannel trousers and what looked remarkably like cricket boots. And around his shoulders was draped an off-white, heavy, ribbed v-neck sweater, with blue and yellow stripes around the neck and cuffs.

'Who is it?' a slightly bewildered Sarah asked Bloom.

'Oh, don't you know?' Bloom raised his hands in apology. 'I'm sorry. I've never been quite sure how well or how long you and David have known one another.' He looked across towards the impressive, angular figure which had now made its way into the room and over to where the drinks were being served. 'That, my girl, is Jonathan Peterson, idol of British publishing and David's editor at Crowther's, his London publisher.'

'My God. Is that him?' Now Sarah remembered David going on about Jonathan Peterson. About how he was a brilliant editor, and yet how he seemed obsessed with creating an image for himself of calculated eccentricity. This was the man who feather-dustered his bookshelves while you sat in his office trying to hold a serious conversation about wholesale changes to your manuscript, or what the jacket illustration should be.

Yes, she knew all about Jonathan Peterson all right. David, with his great admiration for Peterson's talent and his irritability with the man's contrived eccentricity, could never make up his mind as to which was the stronger feeling. He would veer dramatically between genuine respect and equally heartfelt loathing.

Peterson, from a wealthy Oxfordshire stockbroker family, had received the classic young English gentleman's unbringing. Winchester; Balliol College, Oxford. But then, after graduating from Oxford with a first in Classics, he had broken the mould by refusing to go into the family business. He wanted to go into publishing, and that was final. His father tried forcefulness and cajolement by turns. But Peterson's mind was made up, and he wasn't to be swayed. And so the Peterson family had turned their resources towards the task of establishing Jonathan in the exclusive field of British book publishing. After a long chat over lunch at his club with fellow member Sir Hugh McGregor, chairman of the highly successful publishing house which bore his name, Peterson's father had secured for his son a lowly, but much sought after, editorial position within the company. Up to this stage in the story David was scathing. It reeked of everything he despised about the privileged English upper classes. But from then on, Peterson's talent began to shine through. After a few years getting himself a good grounding under the gruff, uncompromising Sir Hugh, he had had no qualms about deserting McGregor's in order to further his career elsewhere.

One of Peterson's chief assets, apart from being very well connected through his family, was his good looks. His strong, angular features; the boyish shock of silky blond hair which often hung down the right-hand side of his forehead and which he would sweep back into place with a characteristic movement of his hand; his slim but strong bearing. It all contributed to his legendary success with women.

One such was Rosalind Stanley, the managing director of Bentley and Dodgson, a small but highly regarded London publisher of quality fiction. Rosalind became infatuated with Peterson and begged him to join the company. This he did, and over the next fifteen years proceeded to perform wonders for them, revitalizing their old-fashioned literary list with the injection of more commercial books, many of them bought in from the United States.

But the break had inevitably come. Peterson had made a stunning reputation for himself, and was continually being bombarded with offers to leave Bentley and Dodgson for one of the larger, more dynamic London publishers. And eventually the financial and prestigious baits dangled before him had been too enticing to refuse.

It was Crowther's, another old-established firm, who finally succeeded in wooing him away from Bentley and Dodgson.

Sarah was puzzled to see Peterson present in New York.

'How come David didn't say anything about Peterson being in New York at the same time?' she said to Bloom.

'Ah, he wouldn't necessarily have known,' said Bloom. 'You see Jonathan does things very much on the spur of the moment. He telephoned yesterday to say he was going to be arriving this afternoon.'

Sarah glanced over to where David was still being held hostage by the indefatigable Cindy Horowitz. She didn't think he had noticed Peterson's reasonably successful attempt at a grand entrance. Or perhaps, knowing David's views on the man, he had indeed noticed him come in, but had pretended not to.

'He looks as though he's making in our direction,' said Sarah, as she spotted Peterson striding across the room towards them.

'Henry. Henry, old chap. How the devil are you?'

His voice was deep and slow. Now he was closer to them, Sarah could also see that he was a little older than his first, distant appearance had suggested. His youthful, sporting apparel couldn't disguise the wrinkles across his forehead, or the crow's feet which now seemed firmly established at the corners of his eyes. Sarah tended to agree with David's impression of the man, at least on first sight. She wouldn't say he looked unconsciously eccentric, but more as though he was painstakingly trying to appear so. He might be the greatest thing to happen to British publishing since Shakespeare. But Sarah didn't think she was going to be able to take him seriously.

'Hi there, Jonathan,' said Bloom. 'So you made it in the end.'

'Yes, yes. You can't keep me away from New York for long.' Peterson glanced at Sarah and smiled. 'Well, Henry, don't keep me in suspense. Are you or are you not going to introduce me to the young lady here?'

'I'm sorry. Yes of course. Jonathan Peterson, may I introduce Sarah Brownlow, friend and er . . . well friend of our esteemed David Dent.'

Peterson turned to Sarah.

'Well, I'm glad young Dent has decided to share his New York experience with someone. It's a great city, but if you don't know it, it can be absolutely awful if you're on your own. Have you been to New York before, Sarah?'

'No, this is my first trip, actually,' she replied.

Sarah had been chatting to Bloom and Peterson for several minutes, when David managed to finally extricate himself from the clutches of Cindy Horowitz and join them. He and Peterson exchanged greetings.

'You didn't tell me you were going to be in New York too,' David said.

'My dear boy. If we were intimate enough to know exactly what one another were doing at all times, people would begin to talk, wouldn't they?' Peterson raised his eyebrows and gave an engagingly mischievous grin. Sarah and Bloom laughed, while David smiled knowingly, as though Peterson always teased him in this way. 'But as it happens you are part of the reason why I *am* here. I've come to discuss with Henry here this wretched new novel of yours.'

'But what about me?' David asked, rather aggrieved.

'You and I have argued quite enough about it already. For the time being, anyway.' He turned to Bloom. 'No, I need another completely biased, money-orientated opinion to supplement my own and convince myself that, when it comes to publishing books, I do know what I'm talking about.'

Peterson cast his gaze around the room, over the heads of his current companions. 'David, where is that delicious woman you were monopolizing when I came in? Ah, there she is. See you all later.' And he was gone. Bloom followed him with his eyes, and smiled appreciatively.

'Say what you like about Jonathan Peterson. And I've said a few things about him in my time. But that guy's got class,' he said.

Sarah wasn't sure that class was quite the word she'd have used. It seemed to cover a multitude of sins for Americans. But now she'd had a little while to take Jonathan Peterson in she had to admit that he had a certain amount of charisma. She imagined he would be excellent company if one didn't take him too seriously. But she found his apparent attitude to women quite fascinating. His reputation for wooing them and then systematically abusing them was puzzling. It was intriguing. Anyway, he was now busily engaged in conversation with the infamous Cindy Horowitz, and was obviously succeeding in giving as good as he got. Sarah and David remained chatting to Henry Bloom for several more minutes. Then Bloom said:

'Hey, listen. I've got a great idea. Why don't the three of us and, say, Jonathan and Cindy all go out for dinner? I know this wonderful Chinese restaurant up on West 65th, near Broadway. You've just got to try it.'

It did seem a good idea. Sarah, for one, was beginning to feel quite hungry. David, who never said no to food, also concurred. So Bloom left them to go and ask the now inseparable Peterson and Horowitz whether they were interested in the proposition.

'God, I hope that dreadful Horowitz woman can't make it,' said David.

'Well, you seemed quite amenable to her a few minutes ago,' Sarah laughed.

David's eyes widened in surprise.

'You're kidding. I couldn't get away from her. It was frightening.' He stroked his moustache, as he often did in his more pensive moods.

'You're looking very thoughtful,' Sarah remarked.

'Oh, I was just wondering what Jonathan was up to.' He nodded in Peterson's direction. 'She just isn't his type.'

'So what is his type?' Sarah asked.

'Oh, I don't know. Nubile young Sloane Rangers mostly, I suppose. He seems to go through an endless stream of them.'

The Shun Lee West restaurant was situated near the Lincoln Center. The decor, sedate though a little frayed, was something of a change from the utilitarian plastics of the restaurants in Chinatown. Its main claim to fame was that it had introduced New Yorkers to the spicy Hunan and Szechuan cuisines which had now become incredibly popular throughout the city.

The five of them had been driven there in the Smithson's chauffeur-driven Lincoln Continental. And as they sped through the steamy New York night, Sarah had watched the glittering Manhattan lights ignite the sky and reflected on how New York never seemed to get dark, never went to sleep. There was something perpetual about it.

The meal was delicious. And the company, apart from the constant, monotonous nasal drawl of Cindy Horowitz, was entertaining. Henry Bloom was in fine form, as was David. But the star of the show was undoubtedly Jonathan Peterson. He held the whole table transfixed and regaled with outrageous publishing anecdotes which he delivered with his inimitable lucidity and style. It wasn't until she and David had got back to Riverside Drive, and David had

79

passed comment, that Sarah realized how much she had enjoyed an evening in the company of Jonathan Peterson.

'You should have seen your face,' David said, as they climbed into bed. 'You were spell-bound. Hanging on his every word. And he knew it too.'

'Oh, don't be silly,' Sarah scoffed. 'You must admit though, he is entertaining.'

'Unquestionably. He's wonderful. You just have to be careful, that's all. Or you'll become one of his victims too.' David gently stroked her cheek. It was the first time he had shown her this kind of affection for several days. 'And we don't want that now, do we,' he said softly. Sarah closed her eyes and then felt his lips tenderly linger on hers. First her teeth began to tingle, and then, after a few moments, she felt her whole body begin to melt. And for the next rapturous half-hour she was lost to another world, a kind of Nirvana, where all her doubts and worries had no place.

EIGHT

Jonathan Peterson always indulged himself by staying at what many considered to be the best hotel in New York. The Plaza, on the corner of Fifth Avenue and 59th Street, was a spendidly elegant building, overlooking the southern end of Central Park. Frequented by celebrities from all over the world, it had a unique international reputation for superb service, style and graceful beauty. And Peterson loved it. He took great pleasure in holding all his business meetings there, usually over tea in the Palm Court dining area. It was a most civilized way in which to conduct business, he always said. And when the accountants and his chairman, Lord Noakes, back at Crowther's in London, balked at his astronomical expense claims, Peterson showed no concern whatsoever. If it worked, which it seemed to have done over the years, then surely it was all worth it.

Peterson had invited David and Sarah for tea at the Plaza two days after Sarah had first met him at Smithson's.

'Wow, look at this place.' Sarah stood in awe, and looked around her at the elegant, sparkling interior of the hotel. 'Have you been here before, David?'

'Yes, I stayed here when I was in New York for a couple of days last autumn. It's very nice.'

'Very nice?' she almost shouted. 'It's beautiful.' She poked David in the ribs. 'I think fame's gone to your head,' she said. 'You've become far too blasé about these things.'

Peterson was waiting for them in the Palm Court. When they had joined him, he called a waiter and ordered some tea. Suddenly, Sarah spotted someone she recognized, a couple of tables away. She leaned forward and stage-whispered to the others.

'Isn't that Frank Sinatra over there, with those two men and that glamorous-looking woman?'

Peterson craned his neck and looked over in the direction Sarah had indicated.

'Yes. I do believe you're right,' he said. And then he proceeded to wave vigorously at Sinatra, who, once Peterson had caught his attention, smiled and casually waved back.

'Do you know him?' David asked.

'Certainly not. Why, should I?' he replied indignantly. David and Sarah both burst into laughter.

'You're just incorrigible,' Sarah giggled.

They sat, chatting and laughing, for nearly two hours. And always Peterson was in control. He moved the conversation from one subject to another, with such dazzling virtuosity, that it was as much as one could do to keep up with him, let alone take the lead. He was unquestionably very attractive, Sarah thought. But she still couldn't quite take him seriously, mostly because he seemed so completely self-obsessed. But he made her laugh. She was only too content just to sit back and be entertained by his sparkling, if self-centred, repartee.

Eventually, she and David got up to go. Peterson got up too, shook David by the hand and kissed Sarah on the cheek. There was nothing remarkable in this. But as he kissed her he placed his hands on her shoulders and gave them a slight, barely perceptible squeeze. Then, as he lowered his hands, they lingered for a brief moment on her breasts. A mere fleeting second it may have been, but it was long enough for Sarah to be certain that it had been intentional. The sudden significance of this gesture, the reality of it, came as something of a shock. She was sure that David hadn't noticed. But she certainly had. For an instant she was stunned. She didn't know how to react. What did it mean? She took the easy way out and smiled blandly into Peterson's amused eyes, before disengaging herself from his grasp. But it worried her. And even more so when, as she and David left the hotel and set off across Central Park, David said:

'You know you were flirting with him, don't you?'

Sarah stopped in her tracks, and a young skate-board enthusiast who had been coming up behind them had to veer violently to his right in order to avoid them.

'What on earth are you talking about?' she snapped. She felt strangely guilty about the little touch Peterson had given her. Almost as though it had been her fault, but surely she had given him no encouragement. She certainly hadn't been aware of it, anyway.

'You probably didn't even know you were doing it.' David carried on walking, leaving Sarah stunned and frowning where they had stopped. She ran to catch him up.

'I think you're being silly, David.' She took him by the hand, and smiled. 'And a bit jealous, too.'

David snatched his hand away from hers.

'Of course I'm jealous,' he said sharply. 'What do you expect? I've seen it happen so many times before with that smooth-talking bastard.'

Flicked on the raw, Sarah's temper flared.

'What right have you got to talk? You and that damned Horowitz woman were thick as thieves at the Smithson's party.'

'We've already had this out. I told you at the time. I couldn't get away from her.'

'Huh. A likely story.'

'This is getting very boring, Sarah.'

'You're telling me.' They came to a bench in the shade of some trees, and sat down. 'Maybe the whole thing's getting boring,' Sarah continued. They were silent for a while. In a large open area of the park in front of them, a group of half a dozen or so teenagers were dotted around an irregular circle of their own making, spinning a frisbee through the air, to and fro between them. Sarah watched it glide and hang tantalizingly above the kids' heads, before it gracefully descended onto one of them as if there were some homing device attached to it.

Sarah was still fuming. This was all too much. On top of everything else; Penny's visitations, whether they were real or imagined; the enigma of David's synopsis; and now this. She was so angry, and frustrated, and confused that she just wanted to curl up into a ball and cry. Perhaps this argument with David was an example of the way their relationship was going. Since she had found his synopsis, she had barely felt at ease with him. And now they were fighting with each other, too. At the moment she no longer knew if she loved him. There were so many things she wasn't sure about. Out of the turmoil of her confused mind came a bright, clear thought. It shone like a beacon on a foggy night. She knew it had to be translated into action.

'David, I think we need a break,' she said.

'Yes.' David paused. 'I think you're right. What will you do? Move back to Cathy and Frank's?'

'I don't know yet,' replied Sarah, 'but we can't go on like this. I'll pack my things straight away. It's for the best, I'm sure.'

They walked back to Riverside Drive in silence. And once in the apartment Sarah went straight into the bedroom and packed her suitcase. Not all the things she had brought to New York were there in David's apartment. She'd left some clothes at Cathy and Frank's place.

Sarah came out of the bedroom, and into the sitting room where David sat with the *New York Times* raised and open. She watched him lower it and look up at her with an impassive stare.

'Where will you go?' he said.

It was funny, but she hadn't really thought about where she would go. It had all happened so quickly, the decision and the deed, that even the immediate future wasn't sharply focused in her thoughts. There was always Cathy and Frank's apartment. But going back there wouldn't solve anything. She really needed to be either on her own, or with people she didn't know too well. There had to be a sort of distance between her and whoever she was with, if anyone, so that her mind was free to follow its own route around her troubles, and not be concerned about those close to her. She knew it was selfish, but it was the only way.

'I don't know where I'll go, David, but I'll be in touch,' she said, quietly. She went across the room, and picked up her tan leather shoulder bag which lay on the sofa beside him.

Three or four minutes later she stood in the clear, sharp evening sunlight, not quite remembering how she had managed to get there.

She began instinctively to walk east, towards Central Park. And it wasn't until she had actually crossed the park that she realized she was making for Cathy and Frank's apartment. She stopped. No. That wasn't going to help anything. A hotel, that was it. At least for to-night, anyway. Luckily Cathy had forwarded to her at David's apartment a cheque from her parents – to keep her going, they said. At least she wouldn't have to worry about the hotel bill, provided she didn't go wild with it. And she had no plans for that. All she wanted to do was think her way out of the maze her thoughts seemed to be trapped in at the moment. She turned and began to head downtown.

Dusk was probably the best time of day in Manhattan, Sarah reflected. It was still warm, of course, but the heat was becoming bearable. And the sun, on its lowering trajectory, shot bright, clean shafts of light along the tunnel-like streets which traversed Manhattan between the East River and the Hudson.

She certainly wasn't making for any hotel in particular. One pretty much in the centre of town would be a sensible destination, she supposed. And a safe one. She weaved her way back across to Seventh Avenue.

Sarah's room in the Taft Hotel, though small and old-fashioned, was nevertheless totally adequate for her needs. And it was reasonably cheap too. The hotel as a whole may not have been overflowing with every flashy, modern convenience known to man, but it had a faded charm. An air of having been once great, and now overtaken by time and technology. But the lobby still proudly boasted its marble walls and its polished wood and brass. Like an old, retired army sergeant who still took pleasure in showing off his medals.

The first thing Sarah knew she must do was to telephone Cathy and Frank. She knew they would understand, and she knew they wouldn't press her. Cathy answered the phone.

'Hi, Cathy, it's Sarah.' Sarah tried to sound cheerful. But she knew she was trying too hard.

'Sarah, what's wrong?' was Cathy's immediate reaction.

It was the first time she had cried properly. The tears streamed uncontrollably down her cheeks and she sobbed as she told Cathy what had happened. Cathy was calm and controlled, as usual. But there was a warmth to her voice which soothed Sarah and made her want to confide in her cousin. She couldn't tell her everything though, however much she would have liked to unburden herself completely on Cathy's slight, strong shoulders. But most of the strange and bizarre things that had been happening over the last few weeks didn't even make sense to herself.

'I don't really have to tell you that you can walk in and out of here whenever you like,' said Cathy.

'Yes, I know, Cathy. Thank you. But I think you understand. I need to breathe a little, if you know what I mean.'

'Sure. Don't worry about it. But, Sarah . . .'

'Yes?'

'We're here when you need us.'

Sarah choked back a sob.

'I know,' she croaked.

'Okay. Take care, Sarah. And keep in touch, huh?'

'Yes I will. Love to Frank.'

Sarah placed the receiver back in its cradle. And suddenly she felt very lonely. As though that very action had severed her remaining links with the only aspects of the hard, faceless outside world that she was familiar with, and loved. For however long it was to be, days, perhaps even weeks, she was now on her own.

But what was happening to her? Was it that she was no longer someone who could believe in happiness any more? Perhaps Penny's death and her own subsequent breakdown had warped her comprehension and acceptance of everything around her forever. Was it that the memories of the past wouldn't let her relax, allow her to abandon herself totally to the passion she had thought she felt for David? It was like an imaginary mirror in her mind which perhaps gave a distorted reflection of occurrences that might otherwise be put down to coincidence. Like the synopsis for David's new book that she had discovered.

. . . *Six months later Benson is in Paris, photographing models for a famous food company's calendar. He recognizes a girl sitting by the fountains at Tuileries* . . .

Was it such a coincidence? There was so much for her to sort out in her mind. And Penny's repeated appearances. What could they possibly mean? Was Penny trying to tell her something? And then, perhaps she was imagining the whole thing. But that was why she had taken this decision, so that she could attempt to fathom it all out. Put it all into some kind of perspective. Sort out the real from the imaginary. And to do so, she had to get away from David. Her row with him had made it a little easier, if anything. Given her the push she needed. Even now, when she thought about it, she bristled with indignation. How dare he accuse her of flirting! And with Jonathan Peterson of all people. But her anger had lost its really vicious edge now, and she was just aware of herself feeling the slightest pang of regret. But she must give herself time, she thought.

Sarah looked at her watch. It was just after seven o'clock.

'Dinner in the restaurant here, I think,' she said aloud to herself, as she lay back on the fairly wide single bed in her hotel room. It didn't seem to be quite the thing, in this part of town anyway, for a woman to go out to a restaurant alone. In Greenwich Village it was probably more acceptable, but that was a long trek downtown and she couldn't really be bothered going that far. And then, of course, there was always the vague possibility of bumping into David. No, all in all, it would be a much better idea to spend the whole evening here at the hotel, and then have herself an early night. She hadn't realized until now, quite how much the emotional strain of the last few hours had taken out of her. She was feeling very tired.

But first things first. She was going to have a bath. A good old-fashioned bath. It would make a change after so many high-speed, invigorating showers that seemed to ty-pify the frenzy of New York life. And, anyway, it would be more in keeping with the Taft's ambience of solid, ponder-ous sophistication-in-decline. Yes, a bath would relax her. Slow down the thoughts that were scuttling around her brain, like frightened mice. Then dinner would satiate the hunger which was just beginning to make its presence felt. And finally bed and peaceful slumber would close the pro-ceedings on a day that had seemed as though it would go on forever. It seemed a perfectly straightforward programme for the evening.

The bath was delightful. Soothing and soporific. And as she lay back in the big, old white bath tub, with its huge old-fashioned shower attachment nestling above the taps like one of those cumbersome old telephones, her mind emptied. It became full of absolutely nothing. And it felt wonderful. Time seemed to stand motionless, with no glimpses of the past or speculative peeps at the future. Just the present, with its perpetual moment. But no easy answers presented themselves to her uneasy mind. . .

She picked up the phone.

'Good morning. Can I help you?' came the cheerfully polite female voice of the hotel operator.

'Can you tell me the time, please?' Sarah asked.

'Sure. It's seven twenty-seven.'

'Thank you.'

'You're welcome. Anything else?'

'Er . . . no. That's fine. Thank you.'

'Have a nice day,' the operator almost sang in just the same way everyone in New York seemed to. But despite its parrot-like, nursery rhyme delivery (you were never under the illusion that this was some heartfelt message), when someone automatically uttered the phrase to Sarah it simply made her feel good and well-disposed towards everyone and everything around her.

The fresh, new day, heralded by the bright sunlight which flooded the hotel room, seemed to sharpen Sarah's appetite. Breakfast was called for. A big one.

NINE

Sarah had walked past the New York Port Authority on several occasions, but had never had cause to go inside. Before she met David she had restricted herself to the confines of Manhattan. And since then, whenever they had ventured outside the city, David had always hired a car. The Port Authority, a huge, sprawling terminus for buses from all over the United States as well as Mexico and Canada, had something of a seedy reputation. And perhaps fittingly it was situated in one of the less salubrious little areas of the city. Sarah had been fascinated, on her strolls around the city, to discover how small pockets of poor, run-down New York could be found sandwiched between some of the more fashionable, sophisticated districts. And the area around the Port Authority was just such a pocket. Eighth Avenue around the low forties was not an area one would potter around, out of choice, late at night. Pimps and prostitutes peppered the sidewalks of 42nd Street as well as Eighth Avenue itself. And the whole vicinity was poorly lit when it became dark, compared with the dazzling brightness of Times Square only a block away. But even during the day it wasn't the most appealing of places to be. The odd down-and-out sat dozing on the sidewalk, only to be moved along by a flat-capped New York policeman. Even the pretzels on the mobile snack stands were cheaper. This was something Sarah had noticed on her travels around town. You could always tell how an area rated by the price of its pretzels.

She walked through the front doors of the terminus building, put down her suitcase and looked around her. It was frightening. The place was so enormous, although that shouldn't have been such a surprise, she reflected, in the land of enormity. Yet she was somewhat surprised by the modern, clinical, airport-like cleanliness and freshness of the place. For some reason she had expected to see old-fashioned ticket booths, the floor covered in litter, old tramps curled up and sleeping on the seats and the smell of urine. But it was quite different. A welcome respite from the sleaziness which pervaded the atmosphere outside. After several enquiries she managed to find the correct ticket booth, bought her ticket and made her way to the gate to which she had been directed.

Once she had descended to the 'engine room' as it were, of the terminus, the actual place where the buses themselves came and went, Sarah found the atmosphere completely different. The sounds of the buses revving echoed and reverberated against the dirty concrete floor and pillars. It reminded Sarah of one of those multi-storey car parks one always found in English town centres these days.

She was a few minutes early, so she sat down in the small waiting area that accompanied each boarding point, and observed the six or seven people who appeared to be waiting for the same bus. Opposite her stood a young man, possibly a student. He had closely cropped hair and was wearing faded Levi's and a cap-sleeved T-shirt, displaying a fine, though not grotesque pair of biceps. He was good-looking too, Sarah observed, with his steely blue eyes and his perfectly shaped nose and mouth. Beside him, propped against the wall was a bright red haversack with various badges and emblems, the trophies of a well-travelled young American, stitched haphazardly across it. He took a packet of Gauloises from his hip pocket and casually lit one. And as he shook the match to extinguish the flame, he glanced at Sarah and smiled. She suspected the dangers of smiling back at him, although that would have been her instinctive reaction on safer, more familiar ground. Instead she turned to look at the elderly, grey-haired black woman beside her. She was a big, buxom woman wearing a very full cotton dress in bright red with a small floral pattern repeated all over it. Sarah's attention had been partly drawn to the old lady due to the fact that she hadn't stopped muttering to herself ever since she had got there. Sarah couldn't pick up any of what she was saying, but she seemed more than a little irate about something or other. And now the clock above their heads showed the bus to be nearly five minutes late, the woman suddenly stood up, paced over to the exit still muttering, peered out expectantly for the bus, and then strode back to take her seat again.

Beyond the funny old muttering black woman there was a middle-aged Hasidic jew, sitting bolt upright, with his hands perched deliberately on his knees. He had a thin wispy beard and ringlets which dangled loosely on either side of his head, and he was wearing a black homburg hat and a long black tail-coat. He looked to Sarah as though he had been caught in a time warp, transported in time from turn-of-the-century Russia, and set down here, in the middle of 1980s New York. She had seen a few of his kind around the city. And most of them were dressed in very similar style. It beats me how they can bear to wear all that lot in this heat, she thought.

She pondered, with a certain amount of pleasure, on what a motley little gathering this was and how it reflected something of the colourful, cosmopolitan diversity that actually constituted New York City. It quite excited Sarah to be among real New Yorkers again. Since she had been with David she found she had lost touch a little with the city's street life. All this hobnobbing with the sophisticated literary and show business elite was great fun. There was no doubt about it. She thought she probably enjoyed it more than David who, although he played his part in it quite skilfully, felt it all to be somewhat alien to him. And she had to admit that there was something synthetic and false about it. 'A charade', David had called it. She was tempted to agree with him. All those powerful, influential, rich socialites playing at being powerful, influential and rich.

The bus finally arrived about twenty minutes late. By this time the crazy old black woman in the floral dress had worked herself up into such a frenzy of agitation that the poor bus driver looked set for an angry earful. But surprisingly, once the doors of the bus opened, the old woman who had bustled her enormous bulk to the front of the queue, silently showed her ticket to the driver and then went on to occupy a whole double seat four or five rows back. Then she started muttering again.

Once they were out of the city, spacious expanses of sky substituted the crowded jumble of the Manhattan skyscrapers. Sarah could actually see an unbroken horizon for the first time since they'd got back from Long Island.

As the bus clattered north, leaving behind the inimitable Manhattan skyline shrouded in a hanging mist of smog and heat haze, Sarah smiled to herself, and wondered what the hell she was doing heading towards Bridgeport, Connecticut. And Andrew Simpson.

He had been obviously surprised when she'd called him from the Taft. But he'd hidden it well. Very well. With his effortless charm and quiet confidence, Sarah had almost been convinced that he fully expected the call. That it had been a foregone conclusion.

But as far as Sarah was aware, the decision had been a purely impulsive one, and as such, bore no relation to the conflicting, confusing thoughts flying around her head. Yet in many ways, it made sense. It was probably good for Sarah to get out of the city again – away from the temptation of going back to David, out of dejection and loneliness, before she had worked things out.

As she stared out of the bus window dirtied by the dried evidence of careerings through roadside puddles, Sarah was almost unaware of the beautiful countryside hurtling by her. The monotonous drone of the engine made a soporific, unconscious backdrop to her thoughts.

Her mind drifted, eventually settling again on the subject of why she had suddenly decided to go and visit Andrew Simpson. But she had enjoyed the spontaneity of this impulsive venture. And spontaneity was something which became missing in a relationship after a while. When the early spark of novelty and uncertainty had gone, the liaison turned into something else. Or it didn't. You either came to appreciate different things about one another, which substituted for the fickleness of initial infatuation, or the whole thing disintegrated in the face of unadulterated boredom. She wasn't bored with David. No, she was sure she wasn't. It hadn't happened like that with him. As a relationship it had seemed to grow and flourish, rather than wilt towards an inevitable demise. And yet . . . and yet . . .

Even so, when David entered her thoughts now, there was a clear, unmistakable prick of pain and yearning in her heart.

The bus's engine droned on. The freeway fell away behind and loomed identically before them. The scenery to the side changed little and became a mesmeric blur. Sarah's stare through the window beside her became a mindless trance, and her brain began to empty. It was a kind of wide-awake sleep. She ought to try and stay awake, she thought. She might miss Bridgeport. But her resolute attempts to prevent herself dozing off couldn't stop her drifting back to her comfortable, unconscious gaze.

At one point Sarah managed to switch her attention from the entrancing sameness of the view to her reflection in the grubby glass. She studied her face, though she had to concentrate closely because the sun was strong, making the reflected image weak. There was a little spot just beginning to emerge next to her nose. Have to do something about that, she thought. Then, as she strained to see beyond her own reflection, her heart nearly stopped. For next to her where no one had been sitting since they left New York, there was a figure. And it took no time for her mind to furnish the image with the features she knew so well. It was Penny. She too was looking, over Sarah's shoulder, towards the window. And she was shaking her head. Slowly. Rhythmically. Her eyes narrowed and her brow furrowed. And still, with a slow, measured movement, she shook her head. Perhaps the natural thing would have been to look round to confirm or deny the apparition. But for a moment she simply couldn't. Somehow, seeing a reflected image gave the whole thing a distance, a detachment she could handle. Slowly, very slowly, she turned her head through one hundred and eighty degrees. Nothing. Just her bag, sitting on the seat beside her, exactly where she had placed it when she boarded the bus.

She turned back to the monotonous scene whisking past her as the bus rumbled on. Now she was very much awake and her mind active. And again she found herself simply trying to figure out why. Why was Penny haunting her? That's what it was. Surely there was no denying it now. But what did Penny want? What was she trying to communicate to Sarah? Was she telling her that there was something she should consider not doing in the near future? It was strange, but Sarah didn't feel so frightened now. More intrigued. And also now, it seemed as though she had an ally in Penny. Maybe that was going too far. But certainly with so much going on around her that she didn't understand, Penny's apparent return, once accepted, had already seemed to have lifted some of the pressure from her. For one thing, those first sightings of Penny had now, in a strange sort of way, been explained, or at any rate justified, by this latest visitation. And, secondly, Sarah felt as though she could now share the burden of her thoughts. As if Penny were an extension of Sarah's own mind: a receptacle to accept some of the mental turmoil that Sarah couldn't handle herself.

Andrew Simpson's house in Bridgeport, though not appearing large from the outside, extended back quite some distance. And so, once inside, it had an intriguing, tunnel-like quality. As one walked through, it seemed to go on forever, with lots of little twists and turns, nooks and crannies, and dotted about everywhere were some of the most beautiful antiques Sarah had ever seen. Simpson had bought the land and had the place built to his own specifications, seven years before.

'I really wanted to get away from those big, bland, open-planned designs Americans seem so keen on. Don't get me wrong, though. I love this country and I love the people. But every nationality has its general weaknesses. And here, I think, it's design sense.' Simpson leaned back in his armchair, and took a sip of his tea. 'But I probably wouldn't like them any other way. I'd hate it if Americans were as conceited and snobbish about those things as, say, the French.'

There had been one room in the house which Simpson had not shown her during the guided tour of his residence.

'Oh, I keep that room locked,' he said, as Sarah tried the door. 'I use it as a sort of storeroom for the less appealing antiques that I hope to shift eventually.' Simpson waved his hand dismissively at the white wood-panelled door, and turned to lead the way down the corridor. 'It's a bit of a mess in there. And really not very interesting.'

After tea, Simpson took Sarah for a walk around the town. The odd wispy, white cloud obscured the sun for brief periods, although it was still very warm. In fact they were the first clouds Sarah had remembered seeing for weeks. And if anything they gave the early evening sky a quality and dimension that long days of endlessly blue skies lacked.

Simpson told her more about what had convinced him to come and settle in the United States twelve years before. He had been divorced from his wife, a sad, tragic woman who had taken to drink soon after they were married, and who continued to make his life hell, until he could take no more.

It was during dinner, which Simpson had prepared with his own hands, that he suddenly said:

'You know, I really loved my wife.' He put down his knife and fork, rested his chin on his clasped hands and stared absently over Sarah's head. 'That's what made the whole thing so unbearable.' He lowered his eyes to meet Sarah's. 'Have you ever watched someone destroy themselves like that?'

'No. Not really,' Sarah replied.

Simpson picked up his knife and fork again and resumed eating.

'It's just heartbreaking. Especially when you care so much, and there's absolutely nothing you can do. I think it would have destroyed me too, if I hadn't ended it when I did.'

'Don't you ever see or contact each other any more?' Sarah asked. She hadn't realized that their conversation would become so intimate and revealing. But she found herself quite moved by Andrew Simpson's sad tale. And in a funny sort of way she was pleased by the revelation, in that it showed a side of him and his past whose existence Sarah had never before suspected.

'No. It had to be a complete break. I had to start a totally new life. I've tried to erase it from my memory,' he said.

'Oh, I'm sorry,' Sarah said quickly, not wishing to perpetuate the reminiscences if they were so painful.

'Don't worry. It's my fault. I'm the one who brought it up. Of course, it's impossible just to pretend that something like that didn't happen. But this place helps. America, I mean. It's the land of fantasy and dreams. And if you're lucky, some of the dreams can actually come true here. In fact they're probably more likely to than perhaps anywhere else in the world.' By this time he had finished eating, as had Sarah. 'Do you mind if I smoke?' Sarah shook her head and turned down his offer of a cigarette. She had never been tempted to take up smoking, although Penny had indulged on occasion. It was one of the few things over which they had had different views.

Simpson lit a Winston and leaned back in his seat. There was both pleasure and wistfulness on his face as he blew the first smoke high into the air above their heads. He was wearing a short-sleeved shirt with small, thin blue checks, and a pair of pale blue cotton trousers. If you didn't look at him carefully, Sarah thought, it might be easy to mistake him for thirty-five or -six. His longish, well-styled hair showed no signs of going grey, or falling out. But it was around the eyes and mouth that the relentless march of middle age was beginning to make itself apparent.

'You've been here for quite a few weeks now,' said Simpson. 'Do you feel you'd ever be tempted to come and settle here?'

'Yes, possibly.' And Sarah went on to tell him of the thoughts she'd had about that subject while she had been in East Hampton with David. About the feeling of space and expansiveness. And opportunity.

Oh, David. It was the first time he had entered her thoughts since the bus journey earlier in the day. And she instantly felt a painful stab of remorse and regret. It was as though she had carried out this whole operation, the trip out to Bridgeport and Andrew Simpson, under a sort of compulsion. The idea of making the gesture had taken over, and she hadn't really been in control. The thought of David snapped her back into the realm of reality. What the hell was she doing here, alone with this strange man? Surely this had been an impulsive mistake that could make things even more complicated and unpleasant than they already were. Perhaps that was what Penny had been trying to tell her. Yes, she must go back. Of course she must. First thing in the morning. Definitely. She would worry about where to go later. Certainly she couldn't go back to David. That would defeat the object. And anyway, he might not want her back. They hadn't parted on the best of terms. But now she had an evening ahead of her . . . and a night in this house with Andrew Simpson to negotiate. And she wondered if his intentions were as honourable as hers now were. Anyway she wasn't sure that she would have slept with the man even if that had been his plan. It had been pure impetuosity on her part and none of the finer points had really been thought about.

Their meal had consisted of scrambled egg with smoked salmon for hors d'oeuvre, followed by trout with savoury cucumber and herb stuffing. And now Simpson presented the part of the meal of which he was obviously most proud.

'I've never tried this before. I hope it's okay,' he said, with a big, boyish grin on his face.

'Mm, crème brûlée. My favourite. It looks wonderful.' Sarah took a small mouthful. 'Oh, my God. It's delicious,' she said with her mouth still full.

'I'm glad you like it. It's something I keep promising myself I'll make. But you know how it is. There are a million things one wants to do, and never gets round to doing them. It makes life that little more interesting, I suppose. The fact that there are all these possibilities to pursue if one wants to pursue them. Even if you don't bother.'

At that moment the candle which had been flickering somewhat weakly, fizzled out. For a split second, Sarah almost panicked. Suddenly the atmosphere seemed to change from one of a relaxed, chatty tête-à-tête to something mildly sinister. Then, as if to endorse her momentary fear, she felt Andrew Simpson's hand reach across to touch her own. Sarah gasped.

'I'm sorry. Did I startle you? I won't bite, you know. Not yet, anyway. You'll have to wait for the full moon to enjoy that pleasure.' Sarah laughed, somewhat reassured but still a little uneasy.

'Oh, don't worry,' she said. 'It's me. I'm just so jumpy

these days.' She paused. 'Er . . . aren't you going to light another candle, or put the light on?'

'Don't you prefer the moonlight, now you've adjusted to it?'

It was true. There wasn't much of it, but what was visible of the moon shone through into the room. And now it was beginning to highlight a few more of Andrew Simpson's features than just his mysterious silhouette. Sarah felt slightly more comfortable, but nevertheless still unsettled. Simpson still held her hand.

'I'm glad you decided to come. And on your own, too.'

Oh dear. This was likely to get very awkward now. Mind you, I only have myself to blame, she thought.

'Are you?' she replied, trying not to expose her nervousness. The only way this whole thing wasn't going to escalate into a bedroom farce was for Sarah to be firm and positive now. She had to make it clear to him that what seemed to be in his mind as the natural next stage in the evening's proceedings, was most categorically not in hers. Not now, anyway.

'You're looking troubled,' he remarked. 'That much I can see.'

'Andrew, I don't think you quite understand.' She stopped and searched for the words to continue. 'It was really lovely of you to invite me here. But I think, perhaps you read more into my acceptance than . . . than I intended.'

Simpson looked bewildered.

'Oh, I see,' he said slowly. He looked down at the table and released Sarah's hand. 'I seem to have made a bit of a fool of myself, haven't I?'

'Oh, please don't say that, Andrew. I'm fond of you. Really I am.' Now she, too, looked down at the dirty plates and dishes before them. And she couldn't quite stop herself saying, 'Perhaps if circumstances had been different . . . who knows?'

'Yes, it can always be different. But, of course, it never is. Things happen in a certain way, and no amount of speculation can change them.'

'I think it might be best if I leave in the morning,' Sarah said.

Simpson looked up in surprise.

'Please, won't you stay for another day or two?' he asked earnestly.

'Don't you think it would make it worse?' She paused. 'And anyway, I want to get back. To David.' As she said this, she realized that it possibly didn't mean much to Simpson. Although he may have suspected that something was not quite right about their relationship, Sarah had never mentioned anything about it, and he had never asked. Nevertheless, her last statement would have confirmed it all for him if he'd had any doubts. Although she wasn't going back to David, it seemed a more reasonable excuse than just the fact that she had made a mistake and changed her mind. That would seem most capricious. She hoped he wasn't too angry with her. She did like him. It was just that this hadn't been a particularly good idea after all. And it was best to rectify the situation before it became too late.

If things had been different, maybe something would have occurred between them. Although recently she had begun to speculate with some concern about how she might be losing touch with her own age group. Andrew Simpson was about double her age. It was strange how, ever since she had been eighteen or so, she had been drawn towards older men. Not always as old as Simpson, it was true, but invariably old enough to have different tastes in music and things like that. But David was different. In many ways he was as mature and grown up as any thirty-two-year-old. But perhaps because he had not yet married and had not been leading a normal, run-of-the-mill life since *The Defector*'s success, he was free of the responsibilities and the mummifying effect wedlock seemed to have on people's sense of fashion and taste. His mind was still fresh and open to the constantly shifting trends around him.

Sarah spent the night in one of the two visitors' rooms. In the morning Simpson saw her onto the bus for New York. He didn't say much.

Sarah hadn't yet thought about where she should go, once she got back to New York. There was a temptation to return to the familiar comfort and safety of Cathy and Frank's. But that wouldn't really help matters. She'd be made welcome, of course. But wouldn't that be running away from the problems? Problems that could only really be sorted out in her own mind in objective isolation. She needed a little time and some space.

And, partly for the same reason, she couldn't go back to David. Not yet, anyway. Not until she had decided or had confirmed to herself whether there was any connection between Penny's appearances and David's new novel.

As the bus jerked and bumped along the freeway towards New York, Sarah gazed mindlessly out of the window, as she had done the day before. She half-expected to see Penny's reflection again, but this time it did not appear. She was going to have to think of something before the bus pulled into the Port Authority Terminal. She couldn't walk the streets all night. There was always a hotel again, she supposed. Yes, perhaps that's what she would do. Another night in the Taft.

She rummaged through her shoulder bag, looking for a paperback she'd been reading before she left New York. She pulled it out, and opened it at her place. But as she did so, something slipped out from between the pages, onto her lap. She picked it up, stared at it, and her heart suddenly leapt. It was a photograph of David and herself, taken by Frank with David's expensive Nikon a week or so before. They were outside the Guggenheim Museum. David was standing just behind Sarah, and the idea had been that he would place his hands on her shoulders. But Frank had taken so long to compose the shot, imagining he was David Bailey or Lord Lichfield, that David had got bored. And just before Frank pressed the shutter release, David had put his hands over Sarah's eyes. Frank had been so busy concentrating on getting the right exposure that he had taken the photograph before realizing what David was doing. It had been a very funny occurrence, especially with Frank going on about how it was surely the end of his career as a professional photographer. And after the photograph was developed it instantly became one of those priceless, captured moments that could be cherished forever. David must have slipped it into her bag while she was packing. She hadn't looked at her book since she'd left New York. That was why she hadn't come across it sooner. She flipped the photograph over. He had written something on the back. 'Come back soon. I love you.'

Oh, David. What a fool she'd been. A damn fool. He loved her. And as she looked at the photograph again, and studied his adorable face, frozen in a spontaneous grin, she knew she loved him too. And that was all that mattered.

Sarah turned the key in the lock and opened the door to David's apartment. She had forgotten to leave the key behind. Perhaps it had been a subconscious gesture, and without being aware of it, she had always intended to return. Who could possibly explain how a confused and angry mind worked?

David came out of the sitting room and stopped dead in his tracks as he saw Sarah. She stood a little uneasily just inside the door and placed her suitcase down on the floor beside her. There was silence for a few seconds. It seemed an eternity to Sarah. They just stood and stared at one another, neither knowing what to say. Then simultaneously they both took a tentative step forward. David smiled. Sarah smiled back. And before she knew it they were wrapped in a passionate, unrestrained embrace. And then, suddenly, David swept her off the ground and carried her into the bedroom, leaving her suitcase standing abandoned by the door . . .

TEN

'Tell me, my child, what is it like to be a real femme fatale?'

Jonathan Peterson was holding court again. This time in one of his favourite restaurants, Orsini's on 56th Street near Fifth Avenue. Peterson liked it because the often drunken stagger three blocks or so back to the Plaza Hotel was just enough to clear his head, 'so I don't throw up all over their priceless furniture and carpet,' he'd said.

'All right, Jonathan. That's enough,' said David without much conviction. It was impossible to stop Peterson once he began careering off on a subject.

'Poor young Dent here was heartbroken. We nearly had a dead Dent on our hands. Killed by his own poetic hand for the woman he had loved and lost. It was very nearly a tragedy of astronomic proportions. Especially for me and cigar smoking, cheque-book toting Henry Bloom. We stand to lose a considerable amount of money and probably our jobs if something should happen to this valuable little commodity here.' Peterson indicated David.

Peterson's jibes could do nothing to dampen the new fire of passion that burned between Sarah and David. It was like starting again, but better. To Sarah, it seemed their love had gone through some kind of test and had come out revitalized, and more confident. Now she felt more sure of David as each hour passed. They would never be apart again, he vowed, and she believed him. Because now there seemed no other possible truth. Their petty differences were completely forgotten, because they had been a mere product of a lack of confidence in one another. While they had been apart, true love had been busy reasserting itself, and now Sarah and David were reaping the benefits. Sarah felt smothered with pure joy all the time she was with him.

He was hers now, and she submitted herself willingly to the notion that she was unmistakably, completely, his.

David was still troubled about certain things. The question of the casting for *Chain Reaction* still hadn't been resolved, and presumably *Call Back Yesterday* was still causing considerable problems. But at least he didn't have to worry about Sarah. They were together again. Whatever happened.

'I don't know why you bothered to return to him, my dear girl,' said Peterson as he beckoned to the waiter to bring some more coffee. 'Look at him sitting there, feeling very smug and pleased with himself.'

David smiled and slid down in his seat. This was all water off a duck's back to him. He knew Peterson far too well to take offence at such comments. 'You've just pandered to the man's conceit,' Peterson continued. 'You'd have been much better off with someone like me, charming, kind, brilliant and utterly devoted to you.'

'Too demanding,' said Sarah. And she laughed. 'Much too demanding.'

'I almost believe you mean that,' replied Peterson, with an expression of mock surprise and horror on his face.

The waiter arrived with the coffee. 'Ah, thank you, my man,' said Peterson. 'Now where were we? Ah yes. Too demanding indeed.' He wagged a finger slowly and deliberately at Sarah. 'You, my girl, are a wicked, capricious, delicious little wench, who could do with a good spanking. Or something worse.' His eyes twinkled with a mischievous sparkle, as he said this. She thought she just caught sight of him winking at her. Better perhaps to ignore his obvious enthusiasm for her company. Now, with David beside her, Peterson's charm seemed to have very little attraction for her, anyway. She had found the man she loved, and nothing was going to be allowed to risk their happiness.

The threatening note arrived two days later.

It was late on a Saturday night. David and Sarah had spent the evening over at Cathy and Frank's apartment.

They had left the Robsons soon after 1 a.m. and taken a taxi back to Riverside Drive. But once inside the apartment David had suddenly decided to go out again to try and get hold of the *New York Times*. Apparently there was to be a piece in there about the hold-up in the pre-production phase of *Chain Reaction*, due to casting problems. David wanted to find out how much of the controversy had been leaked to the press. And whether he was being blamed. But Sarah was a little puzzled. Why hadn't he bought it on their way out earlier in the evening, like he usually did?

David looked slightly uneasy. 'Oh, well the early editions are just all the supplements lumped together. The first part, with all the latest news, doesn't appear until about now. So I thought I'd wait. And anyway, I think I need the air,' he said. 'I've got a terrible headache.'

Now Sarah came to look at him carefully, he did seem quite pale.

'Okay. I'm going to make myself some hot milk. Do you want some?' she asked.

'No thanks.' David shook his head. 'See you soon.' And he was gone.

Sarah went into the bedroom and took off her fashionably baggy white cotton trousers and her bright, multi-coloured, striped T-shirt and donned her pale blue towelling bathrobe before going into the kitchen. But as she stood over the electric hob, waiting for a saucepan of milk to boil, a disturbing thought came into her mind. Where was David going to get a paper at this time of night? As far as she was aware, there wasn't anywhere nearby which was open this late.

Then she thought she heard a noise coming from the direction of the door to the apartment. Sarah didn't take any notice for a moment, thinking it was David, and expecting him to appear at any moment. But there was no sign of him. The milk was beginning to boil now, bubbling its way up the saucepan. She lifted it from the hob and poured the contents into the large mug she had ready. She had drunk hot milk before going to bed every night since she was a little girl. She and Penny both had. And now, even on hot summer nights she refused to break the habit. Perhaps it didn't really help her to sleep any better. But she found the habit a comfort and a continuous link to her past, her happy childhood and adolescence, when Penny was around and they had both dreamed together.

She was curious about the noise she had heard. Perhaps David had forgotten his key. So she took her milk with her and strolled into the small hallway. There on the floor, below the apartment's solid, imposing front door, was an envelope. How very odd, she thought. She went to it and picked it up.

Typed on the front of the envelope in block capitals was simply: SARAH. She took the envelope into the sitting room, put her mug of milk down on the table, sat down and for a few seconds just stared at the stark, single word that seemed to transfix her. What could it be? She was almost frightened. And yet, at this moment in time, there wasn't anything concrete, substantial, to be frightened of. Fear of the unknown. Perhaps.

As she held this envelope in her hands, any fears she had were in her own mind. They could be passed off, if necessary, as figments of a versatile imagination. But something told her that when she opened the envelope, which she was now twirling nervously in her hands, those fears might be transformed into something much more real and tangible.

Whatever the envelope contained, and after all, it could be something completely innocent, she was going to have to face it sooner or later. But the transition from realizing that to actually doing it was not an easy one to make. It needed something of a quantum leap across the labyrinth of her interwoven confusing paths of thought.

She tore into the envelope and unfolded the piece of paper which was inside.

'Don't merely treat this as a threat or a warning. It is simply what will be. There is nothing you can do to prevent what will be. You, dear, darling Sarah, with your dazzling eyes, your rich flowing blonde hair and your deliciously enticing body are a menace to mankind. Or should I say "man"? Fickle and capricious, you hypnotize us, taunt us and then when your whims change with the direction of the wind or the position of the mysterious moon, you discard us like used sweet wrappers. I've known your kind before. But it must stop. Enough. You cannot be allowed to continue to do any more harm to a poor, mistreated, abused breed – the male race. It will happen. Be sure of that. Perhaps here, or perhaps back in England. Wherever you are, I will find you . . . and destroy you. Just like you have destroyed your men. You may think I am mad, and perhaps I am. But that isn't really any consolation, is it? Telling anyone about this won't help you. It will simply accelerate the manifestation of the inevitable . . .'

The note was typed, and not signed. Sarah suddenly felt very cold. She began to shiver, and tears welled in her eyes. She was a child now, frightened by a bullying girl at school. There was no escape route for her fear but through crying. But she must pull herself together. Think. Think. Be logical.

She read the note through again. There was something in the sentence, 'I've known your kind before,' that sounded familiar. She couldn't put her finger on it, but she felt sure she had heard someone she knew use it, or something like it, quite frequently. Could it be David? It might be, but she couldn't be sure. She shivered and shook that thought from her mind. No, that was impossible. What a silly thing to think. But it was certainly someone she had been with recently. It was terribly frustrating. She racked her brains, but it was no good. Oh, why couldn't she remember? The tears began to fall again. Tears of frustration mingling indistinguishably with tears of fear and helplessness.

A noise at the door. This time it must be David. Sarah quickly folded up the letter and its envelope, and stuffed it into the pocket of her bathrobe.

David came in. Sarah wanted to tell him about the note, but he went straight into the bedroom and began getting undressed. I'll tell him in bed, she thought. They got into bed and David began reading from the *New York Sunday Times*, the full bulk of which lay heavily across his lap.

'David,' she began.

'Mm?' he answered absently. He wasn't really listening to her. That was clear. 'Hey, you see this guy?' He tapped the fuzzy photograph of a middle-aged man on the front page. 'Millionaire businessman. Running for Governor of New York. Says he's going to clean up the inner city slums. As if he really gives a damn.' He carried on reading and muttered, 'I've known his kind before. Probably put up by the Mafia.'

And in that ice-cold moment, Sarah's heart almost stopped beating. 'I've known his kind before.' It *was* David who often used that phrase. Sarah remembered now. But surely this wasn't possible. Just a coincidence. She tried to piece together the facts before she drew any definite conclusions. David's temporary departure had been suspiciously convenient, and the reason for it had not been totally convincing. Anyway it was unlikley that anyone else could have got in through the apartment block's front door without a key. An entry-phone system operated there, and someone without a key would have to be let in by one of the residents. And yet sometimes the front door didn't close properly behind you if you just left it to shut by itself. It was possible, then, that someone could have slipped in when David left. She glanced at David. No, no she wouldn't believe it. He loved

because they were situated here in New York. The feeling would undoubtedly be different again if she were in Paris, she supposed.

If Cathy was in her element directing the proceedings, guiding Sarah around these emporiums of designer delights like a coxswain in a boat race, then Sarah herself most definitely was too. She was never happier than when shopping around for clothes. She was aware, of course, that she had the advantage of suiting virtually any fashion currently in vogue. Her trim figure, fresh complexion and beautiful hair were the stuff of which models were made. Or so many commented, including Cathy, who nevertheless warned her away from it as a profession.

'It destroys girls in the end,' she had said. 'I've seen it happen so many times.'

Still, Sarah was making the most of it on what had unfortunately turned into a sultry, almost sunless mid-August day. She was having a wonderful time trying on skirts and dresses, trousers and blouses. And every time she glanced at Cathy quizzically, as if to say, 'I bet you can't find anything like this on the lower east side at half the price,' Cathy would smile and nod sagely, confirming that, yes, she could. No problem.

They had lunch at The Ginger Man restaurant and from there they walked a little until they managed to hail a taxi which transported them southwards, downtown to the ramshackle, bustling streets of the lower east side. Sarah hadn't ventured there on her own. But now, with Cathy as her knowledgeable guide, she found it absolutely fascinating. Most of the shops sold clothes and shoes, but the atmosphere couldn't be more different to the pricey extravagance and sophistication of their morning jaunt. Here colourful displays adorned the outsides of the run-down old shops, and in the windows themselves the quantity of merchandise on show was the key factor, rather than the style with which it was exhibited. And that was something which Sarah felt characterized the whole place. There was something truthful and honest about it. Polite service and plush fitting rooms were very nice. A pleasure, in fact. But there was no doubt at all that you paid for them. It was all a bit phoney. A charade. Here it was different. You went into these seedy old shops knowing more or less what you wanted. And if you didn't, you shouldn't expect the shop staff to treat you with the endless patience, grace and fussy concern of their uptown counterparts.

Many of the shops sold cheap, tacky goods for the local inhabitants of the area. But there were some places, and Cathy knew exactly where they were, which sold high-fashion designer merchandise identical to the sort of thing they had seen during the morning.

'You know, on a Sunday morning,' said Cathy, as they strolled down Orchard Street, 'you can hardly move down here.' She gave her distinctive little laugh. 'It's really funny to see droves of wealthy Long Islanders and rich young jet-setters from uptown Manhattan jostling with the poor and the down-and-outs from around here.' And then realizing what she had just said she added, with a humorous glint in her eye: 'My interest is a purely professional one, of course.'

They took a taxi back uptown. In the excitement of the day's frenetic scurrying about, Sarah had managed, somehow, to push to the back of her mind the unenviable situation which faced her when she returned to Riverside Drive. How should she treat David? What should she say to him? Here she was, her life, yes her own life, possibly in serious danger, and she was frozen. Not able to move or act. To say anything to anyone. Supposing it *was* David who had slipped the threatening note under the door. Who else would believe her bizarre suspicions about him? It would just be put down to her mental instability over the last year, since Penny's death. It even fleetingly crossed her mind, as she sat beside Cathy in the taxi now cutting its way across town, that perhaps she was mad. But she had firmly held the belief

116

that if one suspected one's own madness, it was as good as confirming one's sanity.

Yet for all her genuine abandon and wholehearted enjoyment during the day's frenzied activity, Cathy, it seemed, suspected something was wrong.

'There's something troubling you, isn't there?' she said softly, as she looked intently but warmly at Sarah. 'I've been watching you carefully all day. You've been having a good time. I'm sure of that. But I kind of felt it was all hiding something. As if you were pushing something away. A thought. An idea. A problem. Is it still David?'

Oh, how she wanted to confide in someone. Share the burden, and get an objective view of the situation from someone who nonetheless cared and understood to some extent. And yet, was it really possible to be objective about the whole thing? God, Sarah didn't know. She didn't know at all. The strange thing was that she could hardly believe what was happening herself. The whole episode was so incredibly far-fetched that it just didn't seem the sort of thing that really happened to people. And if it did, she never, for a moment, thought that it would happen to her.

And so her paralysis, her inability to do anything about it all, was due, not just to fear, but to her own disbelief in her predicament. And it made her feel horribly alone again. More alone than since she had first come to the cold, uncompromising realization that Penny was never again going to be part of her life. And yet now, ironically, Penny had entered the scene again. Several times. Sarah almost wished she would make another appearance. Just so that she knew she was there. Warning her. Guarding her. Who knew, perhaps she would even communicate with her?

The trouble was that Cathy was so shrewd, so wise and perceptive, that it was almost impossible to hide anything from her. But she would never press Sarah. She would make an observation, and that was it. If you wanted to tell her about it, she would listen. If not, that was fine.

117

And Cathy didn't press Sarah now. Sarah chewed at the side of her mouth, and made circling patterns on her leg with her forefinger. And then she muttered croakily:

'Oh, don't worry. We'll work something out.'

No one at all had known about her visit to Andrew Simpson during that brief period away from David. She and David had agreed they would never ask one another what had happened in that day and a half of their lives. And Cathy and Frank knew that if Sarah wanted to tell them, then she would. So that was another secret she was harbouring right now, too. She didn't like secrets: they made people too insular and detached. They cut you off. And yet, on occasions, they were necessary.

Sarah tiptoed into the apartment laden with three large carrier bags. *Tiptoeing*, she thought. This is ridiculous. How much longer was she going to be able to sustain this charade? It was just crazy. And if she wasn't mad already, surely it wouldn't be long before she started cracking up . . . again.

No, she'd had enough. She was going to confront David here and now. And damn the consequences. If she had nothing to fear from him, then a wonderful, passionate relationship might be destroyed for no reason at all. And should all her worst suspicions be confirmed, well, she could always run. And anyway, he wouldn't murder her on the spot. He couldn't. It would be too obvious. He would have needed time to plan it. And she had the advantage of surprise on her side. She went back a few steps to the apartment door, opened it and left it slightly ajar. Just in case. Then she deposited her bags in the bedroom.

She stood at the closed door of the sitting room, and took a deep breath. Then, involuntarily, she swallowed hard. It sounded so loud in her head that she was sure the whole apartment block were certain to hear it. But when she boldly opened the door and strode purposefully into the room to find David seated on the sofa, her resolve weakened as she saw his face. He looked dreadful. Pale and gaunt. And he was staring blankly at the floor in front of him.

'David. What is it?' she asked, keeping her distance for the time being. 'What's wrong?'

He looked up slowly until his eyes met hers.

'It's my mother,' he said. 'She's had a heart attack. I got a cable from my father around lunch-time. She's in hospital, but she's bad. Very bad.'

Those certainly looked like tears in his eyes. Though she couldn't be sure of anything any more. But he looked so forlorn, so lost and unhappy. Sarah went and sat beside him.

'Are you going back now?' she asked.

'I couldn't get hold of you. I didn't know where you'd be.' Then he paused. 'Yes. I'm catching a nine forty-five flight from Kennedy, this evening.' He looked lingeringly at his watch, as if the time it showed was failing to register in his mind. He cleared his throat. 'There's a car coming for me in about twenty minutes.'

Now Sarah noticed David's two suitcases standing over by the table.

'Do you want me to come with you?' she found herself saying, without really knowing why. David placed his hand on Sarah's leg and squeezed it gently.

'No, love. You stay here. I'll call you when I know more. I have to come back anyway. There are still lots of things left unresolved here.'

The car came on time and suddenly Sarah was alone.

She called the Robsons and told them what had happened. They immediately suggested that she go back to stay with them, at least until there was more news. She knew that was the sensible thing to do. It was certainly the safest, but something made her decline the offer. Although it went against every scrap of common sense and rationality, she wanted to be on her own. It was as if she was intent on facing anything that was to come her way, head on. There was nothing really brave about it, she thought. It was something akin to the 'charge' mentality in battle. A kind of mindless resignation to whatever the consequences of her action might be.

ELEVEN

That night she read for the first time since they had returned from the East Hampton trip. Since then she had had neither the inclination nor the time to sit down and read. No, that was rubbish. Of course she'd had the time. It was just no good sitting down with a book, however good it was, if your mind was being torn apart by other things. But as she sat curled up on the sofa reading an old Barbara Pym novel her mother had recommended before she left England, her mind felt refreshingly open and clear. As though it had decided to begin again. Erase the confusions her conflicting thoughts had imposed on her, and face everything from a brand new starting point.

Now she had got into it, the book was certainly helping to relax her mind. The style was easy and the story undemanding. And although it was set in London and not in the depths of the English countryside which Sarah had known all her life, it still made her feel a little homesick. She hadn't really thought much about England as a place since she had been in New York, which in a sense was a good thing. It had, she supposed, been one of the primary objectives of the trip to distance herself from her home and its connotations of the past.

She glanced at her watch. It was nearly a quarter past eleven. 'Time for bed, I think,' she said aloud. She picked herself up off the sofa and, carrying her book with her, made towards the bedroom. Suddenly the silence was punctured by the telephone ringing. A long, piercing ring followed by a pause, and then another ring. There wasn't really any cause to be frightened. It was probably Cathy or Frank calling just to see how she was. Or perhaps David had missed his flight. But somehow she didn't think it was.

These days it seemed that every tiny, apparently inconsequential thing that happened to her had sinister implications. That was why she was so terrified to do or say anything any more. She stood motionless for a few moments, every shrieking ring slicing through her like a butcher's knife. Why won't it stop? she thought. Oh, please make it stop. But she soon realized that the only way it was going to be silenced was for her to pick it up. She took several slow paces over to where the telephone stood, on a small table by one of the armchairs. She chewed at the inside of her mouth. She picked up the receiver and put it to her ear. Silence. The tension was unbearable.

'Hello?' she croaked. There was someone there all right. She heard the caller take a deep breath and then swallow heavily. Her voice wavered as she said: 'Hello. Who is this please?' Still silence. She wanted to put the phone down, but something stopped her. Fear? Perhaps it was. At any rate she was petrified into inertia. She just couldn't move. Then she heard a slight muffling, as though something was being placed over the receiver at the other end. Then the voice.

'This is just to let you know that I'm still here. I haven't gone away, and I haven't forgotten my promise to you. I doubt whether you'll even make it back to England. And there's nothing you can do about it. It's going to be great fun, Sarah.' There was a click followed by the endless monotony of the dialling tone.

'Hello. Hello!' Sarah shouted, even though she knew there was no point at all.

She put the receiver down again into its cradle and slumped into the armchair. It was a man's voice. That much was certain. But it was so distorted by the muffling that she had only barely been able to make out the words, let alone deduce whose voice it could be. But as she attempted to play the call back in her mind like a mental tape recording, it struck her that the accent was probably English. It seemed an obvious thing to be able to remember. But the fifteen seconds or so it took for the man to deliver his words seemed as fleeting now she tried to remember them, as they had eternal at the time of the call. It was difficult to reconstruct the sound of the man's voice when she had really been concentrating on what he was saying. Of course, it had all been so unclear that she could never be totally sure that it wasn't a faked English accent, or even a refined American one which could sometimes sound very similar.

Sarah's first thoughts about the culprit's identity actually brought a wave of joy washing over her. Well, it couldn't possibly be David, could it? He was sitting comfortably in the first class compartment of a Boeing 747. Wasn't he? She sighed heavily. She supposed it wasn't necessarily true at all about his mother's heart attack. She had never seen the cable itself, and she hadn't been around when it allegedly arrived. It proved nothing. Nothing at all. He could have been lying about it all. So David was still under suspicion, which meant that she still couldn't tell anyone else about it, especially the police.

. . . Being a psychopath, Benson has no feelings of remorse or comprehension of morals . . .

The first thing was to lock all the doors and windows, she thought with a new-found purposefulness and determination. This she did, leaving the bedroom windows until she had made her hot milk and carried it into the bedroom with her.

Sarah placed the steaming mug on the bedside table and was about to start getting undressed when she happened to glance up at the large mirror on the ornate dressing table. Scrawled in big block capitals with lipstick, her own lipstick, which she had brought with her but had hardly used, were six words:

HOME IS WHERE THE HEART IS

Sarah gasped sharply, and almost knocked her milk over. Oh my God, she thought. He's in here. Here in the apartment. David. It *had* to be David. He was the only one who

123

could have got in, for she had seen no sign of the locks being tampered with. Surely she would have heard someone if they had broken in? But no, that didn't prove anything. It was a rented apartment. She wasn't even really sure who it belonged to. Anyone might have got hold of a key. And surely, if David were the threat, he wouldn't do anything as obvious as announcing his presence by daubing lipstick all over his own mirror? A double-bluff, perhaps? Or perhaps David wanted her to know he was here. Waiting for her. Watching. If he was a psychopath, like the one in his new novel, who knew what strange ploys his warped mind might concoct. Yet surely David could not be the caller. Why should he harm her? He loved her. She knew he did.

She looked up at the mirror again. *Home is Where the Heart is.* Suddenly a memory clicked into place in her mind. 'Home is Where the Heart is' was the title of a Gladys Knight and the Pips song that she and Penny had both adored, and had played incessantly on the hi-fi at home. This *had* to be Penny's work.

She had already accepted Penny's return as a fact of her life. And when she thought about it, it wasn't really any more bizarre than any of the other things going on: the telephone call, the letter and David's mysterious new novel, to name those uppermost in her mind. In fact, she had almost been looking forward to Penny's next visitation. She was only sad that she hadn't been able to communicate with her. Or should it be 'it'? Because since Penny or her ghost, or whatever it was, wasn't real, there was no danger in confiding in her.

'Oh, Penny, where are you? Won't you come and talk to me like you used to?' she said to the ceiling. She got undressed and sat up in bed and sipped her milk. A skin had formed, but she didn't mind. She was used to it. She stared at the mirror and the words daubed untidily upon it. Somehow it appeared as a kind of protection, for tonight, anyway. Like some magic incantation, in Sarah's mind, it cast a spell which would keep her safe from danger. It reminded her of those Hammer Horror movies where garlic was hung round the edges of a room to keep out vampires.

But what could it mean? She studied it carefully. Was it a warning to go home without further delay? Was that where safety really lay? Was it home where love waited for her? The love of her parents and friends, certainly. But what about David's love? That was another possibility. In a few hours David would be *home*, or so he'd led her to believe. Perhaps that's what it meant. Maybe David was telling the truth after all. Oh why did it have to be so ambiguous? Why couldn't something definite emerge for a change? So that she could be sure of something for once. It was just like Penny. She'd always loved riddles. Cryptic riddles that used to drive Sarah round the twist sometimes. Penny had been brilliant at crosswords, something Sarah could never be bothered with. She felt a sudden flash of anger. Anger at her dead sister. It was a strange sensation.

But it was the possibility that Penny was substantiating David's story about his mother's heart attack that attracted Sarah most. It was what she most wanted to believe. Any sign to suggest that all was well as far as David and herself were concerned, and she would grab at it. She didn't mean any harm to Mrs Dent, of course. But she had so cherished his touch, so adored the love-look in his eyes which seemed to reflect and acknowledge her own, that the notion of it all being the cynical deception of a madman would simply destroy her spirit. Penny's death had caused her to ask the same questions everyone asked after a tragic bereavement. Why me? Will I ever be happy again? Meeting David, she had begun to believe in life again. She had even dared to think that, yes, happiness could be hers once more. He had wanted her, and yet he hadn't pressed her, suffocated her beneath a pillow of worthless soggy clichés and compliments. He had just been himself. Honest and genuine. And Sarah had found it intriguing, almost moving. It was certainly refreshing. She wasn't used to such sheer sincerity from men. But now she was being forced to question all that openness and ingenuousness. It gave her a cold, empty pang in her chest and a sick feeling in her throat.

When Sarah awoke the following morning the words on the mirror had vanished.

As she prepared a light breakfast of cereal, fresh orange juice and coffee, she thought about what she could do that day. She hadn't really been planning very much on a day-to-day basis recently. There had been the shopping extravaganza with Cathy the previous day. But apart from that, nowadays she found herself drifting from one day to the next without much sense of purpose. She and David had virtually done the whole tourist bit. But hadn't she read something a few days before about a special exhibition of Edward Hopper's paintings at the Whitney Museum? She liked Hopper's work, and although the Whitney owned more of them than any other gallery, since it wasn't particularly large, it couldn't display many of them at any one time. So occasionally it would drag them out of the vaults, call back the ones that were out on loan and put on a spectacular exhibition of the great man's art.

And anyway, she was damned if she was going to stay closeted in the apartment on her own out of plain fear. If anything, she would be safer out in the open, in daylight, with thousands of people all around her.

The telephone rang out.

Sarah froze, as she had done the night before. But now, of course, following last night's mysterious call, she had much more reason to be frightened.

It was on the fourth shrill ring that Sarah nervously picked up the receiver.

'Yes. Who is it?' she asked tentatively, her voice shaking. There was a moment's silence which seemed an eternity.

'What a strange way to answer the telephone, my dear,' came the quizzical reply at the other end. Sarah's heart leapt with sheer relief.

'Jonathan, it's you.'

'Well of course it's me, you silly girl. Who else would be so concerned for your welfare at this difficult time than your dear, devoted Jonathan Peterson?'

'It isn't very funny,' she said seriously. 'Apparently his mother's quite bad.'

But Peterson wasn't to be reprimanded.

'Oh, poppycock,' he said. 'He told me the same story. But I didn't believe him. It's undoubtedly another woman, my sweet nymphet.'

'You're just impossible.'

'Never mind about that,' Peterson replied dismissively. 'The important thing is that I am completely at your disposal until your elusive lover returns.' He paused. 'If he returns.'

That voice, distinctive as it was when heard normally, might well lose some of its unique tone when muffled and disguised at the other end of a telephone. And, of course, it was English. No possibility could be ruled out. But she barely knew Jonathan – surely it could not be him.

'Well, that's very kind of you, Jonathan. I'm flattered. But I thought I'd spend today, at any rate, on my own.'

'Doing what?' came the instant, rather abrupt reply. It was so abrupt, in fact, that Sarah was caught somewhat off her guard. She hesitated for a second.

'Er . . . well actually I was going to the big Hopper exhibition. The one that's just opened.' Sarah knew her reply must have sounded tentative and unconvincing. And it left her wide open for being dictated to by someone with Jonathan Peterson's confident and forthright personality.

'Perfect,' he said. 'Perhaps his style was a little puerile at times. But then I suppose he typifies a puerile nation. Never mind. I shall swallow my artistic snobbery for the day and accompany you to the Whitney Museum.'

Sarah had to laugh. She couldn't stop herself. He talked such nonsense most of the time, but he knew it. In fact, he'd made an art of it. A day out with Jonathan Peterson might be a good idea after all. She could do with cheering up. And, just in case, she could do with some masculine protection at her side.

They arranged to meet outside the museum at eleven-thirty. Sarah left the apartment on Riverside Drive early and prepared to take a slow stroll through Central Park. The day that greeted her outside was a superb one. Clear, clean and hot, but without the suffocating humidity that had become a monotonous, endless drain on Sarah's energy over the past few weeks. The sun had climbed to its majestic perch in the cloud-bare sky, and there was even the faintest whisper of a breeze agitating the trees in the park.

Sarah knew her way across the park quite well now. She didn't get so confused any more by the labyrinthine complex of paths that wove their way along and across it. With a little time to spare, she decided to go via the zoo, apparently one of the oldest in America. It wasn't yet open, so she found a secluded bench beneath the shade of some trees and sat down to reflect a little.

Suddenly there was a rustling behind her. Her heart jumped and she spun around on the bench to see what it was. But all she saw was a small branchful of leaves, waving limply after being disturbed. She watched it, as though entranced by a hypnotist's swinging watch, until it became motionless again. There was nothing and no one else to be seen. Sarah got up quickly and made her way to where there seemed to be more people around. She kept to the main paths until she was through to the other side of the park, and then walked another block eastwards to Madison Avenue.

Peterson arrived about ten minutes late.

'I never apologize for being late,' were his first words. 'But I needed an excuse to give you these.' And from behind his back he suddenly produced a beautiful bunch of red roses.

'Oh Jonathan, they're lovely,' gasped Sarah.

'I'm afraid I have to own up, my dear girl. They are something of a bribe.'

'A bribe? What do you mean?'

'Why, in order to ensure that you have lunch with me, of course,' said Peterson indignantly.

'And why shouldn't I have lunch with you?'

'Why indeed.'

When they left the Whitney Museum, Peterson hailed a taxi which whisked them off through streets bustling with lunch-time activity, to the Four Seasons restaurant.

'Ah, Mr Peterson. Nice to see you again,' said the head waiter, grinning widely when they arrived. They were shown to a table in the Grill Room, Peterson with his long deliberate strides easily keeping up with the busy, mincing quick-step of the head waiter. Sarah had to break into a run at times to keep pace with them.

'I can thoroughly recommend the duck,' said Peterson when the menus came. 'It is never less than excellent, and has been known to send poor unsuspecting customers into paroxysms of ecstasy.'

'I don't know about that,' said Sarah. 'What am I going to do with these roses?'

Peterson called over a waiter and had him place the flowers in a vase of water on the table.

Around them, the restaurant bustled and murmured its way into the afternoon. Waiters pranced about, from table to table, with positive, purposeful strides and an air of determined concentration. Publishers courted authors, literary agents courted publishers and businessmen courted their secretaries. But whether the circumstances were business or pleasure, Sarah got the feeling that an awful lot of wheeling and dealing was going on. On a table to their right she could overhear two men, one an attractive, slim, thirty-or-so-year-old, the other a short, plump, balding chap in his early fifties, hurling figures and sales chatter at one another. God only knew what they were talking about. In a sense it didn't matter. It could have been anything. The monotonous machine-gun-like exchanges seemed to reduce all business and businessmen to a stereotyped mould. It sort of made them inhuman. Almost like robots. And it totally dissipated the pleasure one could enjoy in having lunch. It was just an extension of these men's working mornings. A high pressure bridging of the gap to the afternoon.

Sarah glanced up at Peterson, and was embarrassed to find him staring quite intently at her. And was that a smirk on his face? Or just a smile? She looked away quickly. He was making her feel a little nervous. Nervous enough for her to ask one of those ridiculously obvious, silly questions you ventured when you were with someone you didn't know very well, and there was an awkward pause in the conversation.

'So you come here quite a lot then? When you're in New York?' she heard herself saying. And she cringed inwardly at the stupidity and pointlessness of her statement. Peterson didn't answer her. And that made it worse. She really was feeling quite uneasy now, and she had to look away from him again. Out of the corner of her eye she could just catch a glimpse of him, and she was sure that his eyes were still set intently on her.

Fortunately, just as she was beginning to panic, and was contemplating excusing herself to the ladies in order to break the uneasy atmosphere, the head waiter came to take their order. And after he had left them, conversation began to flow between them again as fluidly and unselfconsciously as before. Well almost. Sarah couldn't quite forget about those strange few silent seconds that had chilled her as Peterson had stared at her with that disconcerting half-smile curling his lips.

The wine came – a rotund-bodied St Emilion which Sarah found a bit too heavy for her liking.

Peterson asked her about her future plans concerning a career. If she was interested in publishing, he said, he would ask around the trade nearer the time, to see whether there were any openings for her.

'That's very kind,' she responded. 'I suppose it might be worth thinking about.' Although she hadn't really been planning anything along those lines. It *was* kind of him, of course. But she suspected that a good many high-class Kensington and Chelsea girls fell for that one, and ended up being unbearably indebted to him forever after.

They talked about Cambridge. Sarah expected him to be derisive about it, partly because he was Jonathan Peterson, and also because she knew he had been an Oxford man. Oxford and Cambridge people never did seem to be very complimentary about one another's universities. But he had surprised her.

'I often wish I'd gone to Cambridge, you know,' he said. And Sarah detected a certain wistfulness in his otherwise deep, positive tone. 'Or to any university where my family had not been before. But at that time I was too young to have the confidence to break the mould. I was expected to go to Oxford, and that was that.'

They talked some more. Peterson's voice was softer, warmer and less pompous than she was used to. For the first time she thought she was beginning to catch flashes of what lay beneath his extrovert facade.

They had been sitting there for about half an hour. The hors d'oeuvres dishes had been cleared from the table, and Sarah was awaiting her much-acclaimed duck. Suddenly Henry Bloom appeared beside them.

'Well, well. While the cat's away eh, Jonathan.' Bloom, in a beige, light-weight suit, drew on his fat Havana cigar and blew a swirling cloud of smoke high into the air. Sarah just didn't know what to say. What must this look like? What a stupid thing it was for her to agree to in the first place. But as was to be expected, Peterson was a match for

131

the situation. He always met these things head-on, and then dragged them outrageously and brazenly beyond the point where embarrassment stopped.

'Yes, my dear man,' he drawled in his ponderous, deliberate tone. 'Young Ms Brownlow and myself are at this moment in time, embroiled in a passionate, deliciously lustful affair, and were sure we could lunch here, in this quiet, unknown little restaurant without our intimate secret being uncovered. It seems we have failed.'

Sarah giggled and Bloom gave the wheezy laugh of a heavy smoker. But just as Peterson's brash, outspoken impudence was only the superficial exterior of a complex, intelligent man, Bloom's facade of the big-talking, cheerfully extroverted executive quite clearly disguised a sensitive awareness and a not insubstantial amount of talent. So although the two of them teased and taunted one another in the open, Sarah suspected that beneath it all they each regarded the other with the utmost professional respect. Bloom turned to Sarah.

'Did David get hold of you in the end?' he asked her, before another long draw on his cigar caused the ash on the end of it to glow bright red. Sarah was puzzled.

'No,' she replied. 'Should he have done?'

'Well, it's just that he called me at the office, just before lunch. Said he'd tried you at the apartment, and there was no reply.'

'What did he say? How's his mother?' she asked, a little warily.

Bloom took a step closer to the table in order to move out of the way of a waiter careering towards him, laden with plates and dishes of steaming food.

'Well, apparently it's nowhere near as serious as he first thought. I think he's a little annoyed with his father for panicking him unduly and interrupting his trip.'

'So when is he coming back here? He is coming back, isn't he?' Sarah asked.

'Oh yes, yes. In a day or two he said,' Bloom replied, absently. Then he stopped for a moment, and looked thoughtful. 'You know, those transatlantic telephone lines really are great these days. I remember fifteen or twenty years ago, if you called London you could hardly hear the guy at the other end. But like when David called today, it was as though he was telephoning from just around the corner.'

Sarah tried to disguise her shiver as Bloom said this. But not much escaped the eyes of Jonathan Peterson. Those all-seeing eyes that burned through that contrived exterior. The only clear evidence of the mysterious man that lay beneath the surface.

'Are you cold, my dear?' he asked. But he said it with that knowing half smile of his, as though he knew full well why she had shivered. As though he knew everything.

'No, I think someone walked over my grave or something,' she replied. And she finished the statement with a weak, unconvincing smile. Peterson turned his attention to Henry Bloom.

'Wasn't that the priceless Beverly Payne I glimpsed scurrying away when you came over here?' he remarked. 'I suppose she's gone to powder that large, rich nose of hers.'

'Don't knock it, Jonathan.' Bloom looked quickly around him to make sure there were no interested parties eaves-dropping. Then he leaned towards Peterson and said quietly, 'If things go okay, I may have a deal for you in the next couple of days on Beverly Payne's third book.' He gave a brief, wide grin and raised his eyebrows.

'What is the book?' Peterson asked dubiously. Bloom shrugged his shoulders and lifted his hands, palms to the sky, in that inimitable Jewish way.

'I've no idea. I don't think she has either. Does it matter?'

'I suppose not. It'll undoubtedly sell on the strength of her name alone. But out of interest it might be nice to have the slightest of inklings as to the sort of book it will be.'

133

Peterson's tone was different, Sarah observed. In a moment he had slipped from the amusing repartee of the sophisticated socialite to the considered musings of a professional publisher. In that moment he was a man at work.

'Oh don't worry,' Bloom assured him. 'It'll be a saga of some kind, that's for sure. To be honest, I don't think she can write anything else.'

After lunch Sarah and Peterson walked for a while, before he went off for a business meeting. Obviously, when he had said he was completely at her disposal, he hadn't meant it literally. But Sarah didn't mind. She'd enjoyed her day so far, although Peterson had been quite exhausting company, and she was perfectly happy to spend the rest of it by herself. Anyway, David might try to call her from England.

TWELVE

That evening David did call. From England? Judging from the static on the line, it sounded like it. His mother had had a heart attack, but it had been a very minor one, and she was just being kept at the hospital for observation.

It was lovely hearing David's soft, lilting voice again. Soothing but sexually arousing at the same time. She felt herself begin to swoon. She wished he was here now. She wanted him. Wanted him there at that moment.

How could her mixed-up mind have contrived to make her doubt David? She felt like telling him all now. The letter; the phone call; the fact that she had seen the synopsis for his novel. She just wanted to dispel all the fear and uncertainty in one wild, impulsive outburst. Like sticking a pin into an inflated balloon. Release the pressure. Be one with David again, as they had been at the beginning. But before she could speak, David said:

'I'll probably be back the day after tomorrow. But I'll call you again when I'm sure. I must go now. My father's calling me.'

And when Sarah put the receiver down she felt herself glowing. She touched her cheek. It was hot. She felt wonderful. Excited, and elated. Just hearing his voice, was all she needed. She was sure it was all going to be fine. Now all she had to do was wait until he came back to get her, to take her away from New York. She wanted to go home, where she was sure she'd be safe. With David.

She looked at her watch. Nine-twenty. England was five hours ahead. That would make it twenty past two in the morning. Why would David be up that late? Sarah had been back at the apartment for over three hours, and David hadn't attempted to call any earlier.

. . . He is fascinated by the uncanny resemblance and has no qualms about pursuing the possibilities of a liaison with this girl . . .

She shook her head and her bottom lip began to tremble involuntarily. Then came the tears. First they welled, shiny and heavy in her eyes. Then they trickled, first tentatively, then relentlessly down her cheeks. As the first stream reached the corner of her mouth, she could detect the sweet salty taste of sorrow; and fear; and self-pity. Still she couldn't be sure of anything or anyone, it seemed. She wanted to be sure of David. Very much. But every turn of events exposed some sort of niggling doubt, however small. In her confusion and uncertainty perhaps she would always be too sensitive to the sinister possibilities of everything that happened. It was a horribly depressing thought. It made her feel helpless and alone. And vulnerable.

David returned from England in sparkling spirits. His mother was well on the way to recovery, and even the problems over the casting of *Chain Reaction* had paled into insignificance. He was full of plans – they should go to Washington, to see Boston and the East Coast. Sarah weakly agreed to what he suggested. She seemed to have had all the emotion wrung out of her by the events of the preceding weeks.

August seemed to linger interminably in the city. The heat and the humidity slowed everything and everyone down. The whole of New York seemed to walk, even talk, more slowly. Several days passed with no threatening letters, or muffled telephone calls. And no visitations from Penny. David was all tender attention to her every mood. Sarah consciously turned her back on the past happenings. She determined to make the most of her time in the city. Maybe it had all been hallucination anyway.

Of course, her feelings about David were all subject to

136

this same process. She *wanted* to be sure of him. Yet when he gripped her shoulders and purposefully pulled her to him, the tiniest thrill of fear would shoot through her body. For that most fleeting of moments, he might almost be about to murder her. But then, as a soft sensual counterpoint to the aggression of his first gesture his lips would touch hers with such sweet tenderness that she would almost faint with pleasure and desire. She was limp and defenceless in his arms. She was his. He could do whatever he wanted with her.

From the outside of the tall, old house in Greenwich Village they could only hear the incessant drum beat and pounding bass guitar reverberating through the heavy night air. It wasn't until Sarah, David, Cathy and Frank plus some other friends of theirs entered past the big, solid front door which had been left ajar, that the warbling tones of Bryan Ferry became obvious.

'Oh great, Roxy Music,' Sarah muttered excitedly, as she followed Frank up the stairs, stepping carefully over joint-smoking, liquor-guzzling New Yorkers. Most of them seemed to be already completely out of their heads. And it was only about ten-thirty.

'Aw come on, man, you know that's crap. It's gotta be John Glenn and Reagan, the spaceman versus the cowboy,' said one of them, a balding red-headed young man with a wispy beard and a revolting tartan shirt. Then he passed his fat, meticulously-rolled marijuana joint to the older, quite conservatively dressed woman he had been addressing.

'She looked old enough to be his mother,' Sarah shouted into Frank's ear over the din, as they reached the first landing.

'It probably is his mother,' Frank remarked. 'You kind of get pretty strange people at Lois and Clark's parties. Or maybe they're normal folk acting strange.'

137

Dinner in an expensive restaurant just off Washington Square had put the evening off to a good start. The cosy foursome of Sarah, David, Cathy and Frank had been expanded by the introduction of another couple, Bob Carter and his glamorous girlfriend, Sylvia Birch. Bob was a musician, a founder member of the successful American rock band, Stateline. He was now thirty-two, of medium height and slight build, and he had light brown, curly hair and a closely-cropped, almost patchy, beard.

Sarah knew of the band, although having what the music press called 'an American sound', they had never become that popular in Britain. Frank had got to know Carter a couple of years before when he'd landed the job of designing the interior of the rock star's newly acquired New York loft.

Sylvia was a gorgeous-looking woman. There was no doubt about it. Just as heads turned when Sarah walked into the room, her fresh naturalness invigorating the atmosphere around her, so it was with Sylvia. But her beauty had a different quality. There was a voluptuous elegance and sophistication about her that was so tangible you could almost grasp it. She used an abundance of make-up, yet with such subtlety it only enhanced her striking looks, rather than making her appear grotesque. It was the perfect complement to her faultless bone structure and dazzling chocolate brown eyes. And, although she was some two years older than Bob, at thirty-four her figure was as trim and tight as it had been ten years before.

'Hi there, Frank.' A short, plump woman with ruddy, red cheeks and bright, lively eyes smiled up at him.

'Lois! How're you doing?' Frank bent down and gave her a loud, theatrical kiss. By this time the others had caught up with Sarah and himself and he proceeded to introduce Sarah and David to Lois Lane. Yes Lois Lane. Formerly known as Sandy Greenbaum, she had married Oscar Potts in 1976 on the condition that she didn't have to carry his surname through life with her. And what did she want to be called?

Lois Lane. Not that she looked remotely like Superman's famous cartoon accomplice. But Oscar, not to be outdone, had conveniently had his own name changed to . . . Clark Kent. Perhaps in his case there was a faint passing resemblance to his comic-book namesake. He wore the same style of glasses, and he was tall. About six feet seven. But he was skinny and gangling, and didn't really look as though he was about to leap out of a pay-phone booth wearing a cape.

Everybody loved Lois and Clark and their wild, noisy parties. It was permanently open house at their place and most nights it was packed out. They were sort of professional party-givers, and if you mixed in the right circles, you'd invariably end up at one of their extravaganzas sooner or later.

A pungent mist of cigarette and other smoke hung in the atmosphere. People danced; people talked. One odd-looking couple seemed contentedly engaged in serious conversation while comfortably settled in adjacent head-stands. Another man sat in the kitchen sink, with his legs dangling over the side, reading the *Wall Street Journal*.

'Do you always do that at parties?' Sarah remarked to him, as she squeezed past to get to the booze. He lowered the paper and looked over the top of it at her. He gave a wide, ingenuous grin.

'Oh, hi there,' he said. 'I just kind of like the atmosphere here.' And then he resumed his scanning of the latest stocks and shares news.

This was the first party of its kind Sarah had been to in more than two months in the Big Apple. It was so different from the parties she had been to through David's contacts. At the Blooms' party on Long Island, for example, everyone there seemed to be present with some aim in mind. A deal to be finalized; a proposition mooted. But here, at Lois and Clark's, the primary consideration was to enjoy oneself as much as possible. Everyone was so relaxed and natural. The happiness was infectious. Whether it was marijuana or drink induced, or whether it was just a case of feeling beneficent, didn't matter. Sarah embraced the relaxed atmosphere and allowed it to filter through and permeate the innermost recesses of her consciousness. It felt very good.

Although it was one of those parties where inhibitions and shyness had no place, and anyone spoke to anyone, whether or not they knew who the hell they were, Sarah found herself for much of the evening in conversation with Bob Carter. With Bob keeping his hands very tightly round a bottle of Jack Daniels, and Sarah doing much the same to a bottle of Californian red wine she grabbed from the kitchen, they were getting, gradually, very pleasantly sozzled.

My God, she thought at one point. Here I am standing at some wild New York party, talking to Bob Carter of Stateline. *The* Bob Carter. But just like when she had first met David, she was amazed and impressed to find that, apart from his talent, there was nothing very earth-shatteringly special about him. He was just a nice ordinary guy who talked and acted like everyone else, but who just happened to have had fame and fortune thrust upon him. Like David, he was somewhat embarrassed about talking too much of himself and his work. Bob actually seemed genuinely interested in what Sarah wanted out of her life. With the alcohol having the familiar loosening effect on her tongue, she found herself quite openly telling him of herself. Perhaps if she had been sober, she'd have considered what plans she had for the future to be of too little consequence compared with the grand things Bob must have lined up. But one question he asked her had the effect of bringing her to a momentary state of stone cold sobriety.

'And how does David figure in your plans?' he asked innocently.

She hesitated for a second.

'Oh, we'll have to see about that when we get back to England,' she replied, trying to be as vague as possible. Then the conversation moved easily onto other things. She told him how she had been thinking, at one time, of doing a post-graduate course in journalism after Cambridge. But she had been somewhat discouraged by David's unappetizing stories of the struggling life on local newspapers. And everyone had to do their stint there before they were ready for the glamour of Fleet Street and the like. Still, she had a year to decide. So maybe she'd think again.

Sarah looked around the room to see if she could see the others. David seemed to be in one of his serious, animated conversations with Cathy. It was good to see them at it again, just as it had been when David had first come onto the scene. They really did get on so well together. And Sarah felt a warm glow of contentment as she watched them from the other side of the large room. Bob's girlfriend, Sylvia, was dancing frenziedly amid a gyrating clutch of bodies in the room's centre. And Frank had, for the time being, joined the couple of marathon head-stand artists against a wall near where they stood. And that man over by the tall, open window chatting to two, slick-suited executive types. Sarah couldn't believe it. Those famous, full lips. That straight, boyish hair.

'Isn't that Mick Jagger, over there?' she said to Bob. 'By the window.'

Bob looked over to where she was indicating. 'Sure is,' he said. 'That's the man himself. Nice guy, too.'

'So you've met him then?' Sarah was surprised. She didn't see why she should be, though. It stood to reason, since Bob Carter wasn't far out of Jagger's league, himself.

'Yes. We had lunch two or three days ago.' He said this as naturally as though he were talking about his mother. Not the slightest hint of the blasé or the pretentious. For Bob that kind of liaison was a fact of life. That was the sort of world she was included in at the moment, Sarah thought. Fame and money were second nature to some of the people here tonight. Sarah found it all a little difficult to grasp at first. She felt something of an outsider. But as the night

141

went on, she began to feel more at home, more comfortable. She danced, talked and laughed with people she had never laid eyes on before. She and David went into uncontrollable spasms of mirth when Frank sneezed as he was about to snort some cocaine, sending the valuable white powder flying in all directions. The man whose coke it had been, smiled and shrugged his shoulders.

'Aw, let's go and have another drink,' he said. 'I never liked the stuff, anyway.'

They all left the party at around 3.30. The noise and excitement certainly hadn't yet let up. If anything, it was even more lively than when they had arrived. There seemed to be a constant stream of people coming and going. The famous rubbed shoulders with the unknown quite unself-consciously. It didn't matter who they were. These were just people enjoying themselves. Sarah even felt a little guilty about picking out the stars to herself. Because it seemed as far as everyone else was concerned, they just didn't care. She was sure she'd seen Paul Simon huddled by the door in intense conversation with Dustin Hoffman at one point, but no one else seemed in the least bit interested.

Bob and Sylvia's loft was within walking distance of Lois and Clark's place. And so Sarah and David, Cathy and Frank, shared a taxi home. But not before Bob had insisted that Sarah and David come along to the recording studio one day the following week to watch the band working on their new album.

In the taxi Sarah asked until what time the party was likely to go on.

'Oh, probably all night,' Frank answered, shaking his head. 'They usually do.'

When the taxi dropped Sarah and David off at the apartment, it was just after 4 a.m. The sky was already beginning to lighten over the motley jumble of Manhattan's skyline. Neither of them were at all tired. Relaxed and inebriated, but not tired. They stood by the tall, expansive sitting-room window, and watched, transfixed, as the very first shafts of sunlight began their twinkling dance on the surface of the Hudson River. The magic was there again. The silence heavy with emotion and words that wouldn't be uttered for fear of dissipating the potency of the moment.

David eventually led her to the bedroom soon after six o'clock. They began gently, but soon the bittersweet ecstasy of tender, delicate love-making gave way to an animal- like voracity in both of them. But still they didn't tire. Each time seemed to give them new strength, new energy. They finally dozed off at about nine o'clock, carried into a peaceful, sated slumber.

All that day, Sarah and David never got dressed.

THIRTEEN

Washington was something of a disappointment. Still, Sarah was glad to have seen it. After all, one could hardly spend as long as she had on the Eastern side of the United States without venturing as far as the nation's capital.

Time was suddenly running out on them. August had just limply waved its hot and hazy farewell to be replaced by September with its crisper connotations of fall and the beginnings of the year's descent into winter. Of course, the changing months didn't signal any sudden alteration to the current weather. It was still very hot. But Washington was quite as humid as New York. Apart from its importance as the seat of government and all the museums and monuments that went with it, it really was just a provincial, not terribly large city, lacking the thrust and excitement of New York.

Sarah and David still weren't very sure exactly when they intended to return to England. But for certain, it couldn't be later than the third week in September. Sarah was due back at Cambridge at the very beginning of October and she knew she'd need at least a week to prepare herself for the academic year. It was a strange thing to think about now. But Cambridge and the year ahead – a year of extremely committed study – seemed so very far away. Almost in another world.

They had decided to fly to Washington. They could have hired a car and driven there. It would have taken a day without a stop, or two taking it more easily. But the usual panic one gets towards the end of a holiday had set in. It seemed to happen every time, as far as Sarah could remember. You got to your destination and ran around like a lunatic for the first little while. And then, once you had picked up the pace of the place and tuned in to the atmosphere, you began to relax. You became lazy and complacent. And before you knew it, it was almost time to go home. So you ran around like a lunatic again, doing and seeing all the things you'd forgotten about. So to save time, as well as effort, they had flown to Washington.

They stayed there for three days in all. David was in wonderful spirits. He had managed to persuade World Pictures that Gene Hackman was indeed too old to play the lead in *Chain Reaction*. And although no suitable alternative had been suggested, David had convinced the powers that be of the necessity to land someone younger for the part.

As for the other bone of contention currently dominating his professional life, his new book, David said very little about it. This suited Sarah. The longer time went by without it being mentioned, the more Sarah was able, without really being aware of it, to distance herself from David's new novel and any implication it might have for her. He was warm and caressingly affectionate towards her. Whenever he held her, Sarah felt safe again, protected. She had rediscovered the sparkle that had seemed so new and fresh back at the beginning of July. It was astounding how, in those eight or nine short weeks, her life had gone through so many changes. She had experienced previously unscaled heights of desire, love and sexual fulfilment. She had known the dark helplessness that cold fear instilled; the soothing envelopment of togetherness; and the abject misery of being alone, as she had at times even though there were people all around her. But now everything seemed perfect again. The doubts and worries were so far away now, as though they had never existed.

Sarah glanced at David while they sat in the clear, bright sunshine on a bench in Rock Creek Park. He had his nose buried in a paperback he'd bought the day before. It was a Harold Robbins novel, and Sarah had chided him for buying it and for failing to keep up his literary standards.

Apparently it was the first one he had ever read. Frank had jokingly recommended it, not realizing that David would follow his unsophisticated advice.

Now, as she studied him, he seemed to be well over half way through the book. He fiddled with his moustache, pulling at it with his thumb and forefinger. It was the first time she had realized that his hair had really grown quite a bit. David had had it trimmed at an expensive salon off Fifth Avenue three or four weeks after they met. But they hadn't taken much off, and now its soft curls were beginning to fly away randomly from his head. It made him look younger. In fact it was only his moustache that gave the sobering brush of adulthood to a face which, beneath it, was still boyish. It made Sarah think about her own hair. A cursory trim once every four months was all it needed. No costly trips to fancy hairdressers for her. She ran her fingers slowly through the rich plethora of blonde hair now, until she came to a small knot at the ends. Yes, that was the damned trouble with it. Those confounded knots. It didn't seem to matter how carefully or thoroughly she brushed it each morning and bed-time, she still had to endure the dreaded knots. Perhaps it was time for a change, she reflected. Her hair had been this long almost for as long as she could remember. So had Penny's. People were always passing comment about it, and always they were complimentary. Sarah knew it was one of her most admired features. But she couldn't help thinking how childish it was to have hair like that. Well, not childish, perhaps, but certainly girlish. And she wasn't a girl any more. She was a young woman now, into her twenties, mixing with sophisticated adults – novelists and rock stars, no less. She should look the part more. Yes, maybe when she got back to England she would have it all cut off. Show more of her face, and be confident about it. She supposed long hair gave a girl that contrived, shy quality that had often aggravated her in others. Perhaps that was how she appeared. God, she hoped not. Painful as it might be to see her girlhood years fall away from her with the sharp snip of the hairdresser's scissors, her life was moving relentlessly along, changing, growing. She had to move along with it, keeping pace with its shifts and developments. She was really becoming an adult now. It was time she began to look like one.

They visited all the sights: the Capitol; the White House; the Lincoln and Jefferson Memorials; Ford's Theater, where Lincoln had been shot, and the house across the street where he had finally died. They crammed as much as they possibly could into the three days. But Sarah was seeing the trip, more and more, as a kind of duty. Something that should be done, with the minimum of fuss, and the minimum excitement.

They were sitting in a taxi on their way to the National Airport in Arlington, just across the Potomac, for the short flight back to New York. Sarah asked David if he felt the same way about it as she did.

'I suppose you're right,' he answered slowly, deliberately. He turned to look out of his window, and sighed. 'It's kind of nice though, isn't it?' Sarah turned away from him to peruse the passing view from her own side of the taxi. 'It seems cleaner than New York, somehow,' David was saying. 'Smaller, more relaxed.'

'It's got its poor, run-down areas as well, you know,' Sarah replied. 'And one of the highest crime rates in the States.'

'Mmm,' he muttered absently. His mind had obviously moved on to other things. Sarah was used to that now. Sometimes he would stare out at nothing, but in his mind's eye something was clearly being brought into focus: a concept; a character; the twist in a plot. He seemed to pick it out in his brain and highlight it against the busy, confused backdrop of everyday life. And, as on other such occasions, Sarah now thought nothing of it. There was silence for the rest of the cab ride.

The main reason for restricting their Washington trip to three days, was their arrangement with Bob Carter to attend one of Stateline's recording sessions. It was scheduled for the very next day after their return.

The studio, called The Greenhouse, was a fair way uptown. Almost in Harlem. Sarah and David had taken a bus trip around Harlem several weeks before. But they had been continually warned-off walking around it. They took a taxi to The Greenhouse, though even some cab drivers were reluctant to venture far beyond the low hundreds. But the studio was actually very close to Columbia University, in a street just off Morningside Park. They could have walked it, continuing up Riverside Drive (which seemed to go on forever) then turning east when they reached the University, but they decided to heed the warnings they'd been given, and save their legs.

It was about ten o'clock when they arrived, and the day's session had only just begun. They were ushered into the control room. All manner of electronic gadgetry filled the place almost to bursting point. Reel-to-reel tape recorders and cassette decks were about the only things Sarah remotely recognized, apart from the huge mixing console which dominated the centre of the room.

The band stood and sat about in a room adjacent, separated from everyone else by an enormous sound-proofed window. They were doing a 'level' check at the moment, playing short improvised solos on their various instruments so that the engineer could set everything up properly on his side of the glass.

Bob Carter waved to acknowledge their arrival, and when it was the drummer's turn to test his sound levels, Bob placed his guitar on its stand and came into the control room to greet them properly. He beamed a large, genuine smile.

'Hi there. I'm really glad you could make it.'

He introduced them to some of the people in the control room. There was the producer, a man called Michael Cantello, whose longish, straight, jet-black hair and droopy moustache gave him a slightly sinister Latin appearance. But he seemed perfectly amiable. The engineer was actually an Englishman. Phil Stanton had established quite a reputation for himself in British recording circles. Bob had heard about him through the rock grapevine, and had eventually got to meet him during the band's last visit to England. And now, with Michael Cantello's approval, they had flown him over especially to engineer the new album. Sylvia was there, of course, looking beautiful and radiant, even in just a T-shirt and skin-tight faded jeans.

'Sylvia's going to do some background vocals for us later on, if we get that far today.' Bob rubbed her back gently, as he said this, and teasingly looked at her with his head cocked to one side. Sylvia glanced down to the floor, and looked genuinely embarrassed. He turned, once more, to Sarah and David, and in a loud stage whisper said, 'She's got a great voice, you know.'

Sylvia laughed and bit her bottom lip.

'Jesus, Bobby. For heaven's sake,' she giggled.

Bob attempted to explain a little about how a studio worked. David was fascinated. He obviously understood something of the basics. So he had some knowledge on which to build. But for Sarah, the technical jargon was drifting unreachably over her head. It made no sense to her whatsoever. All she was interested in was the music. In this she found an ally in Sylvia, who although she had at one time made her living singing at recording sessions, had never understood all the technicalities of the process.

'I just used to go in there and sing,' she said to Sarah. 'I didn't give a damn what they did to make it come out all right at the other end. That wasn't my job.'

Meanwhile Bob was excitedly explaining the finer points of record production to David, who although he was lapping it up, scratched his head once or twice, obviously lost by Bob's animated babblings.

'Bob, will you get the hell in here?' came a voice over the intercom system between the studio and control room. Bob looked up suddenly at this interruption, like a deer that has heard the snapping of a twig in a forest. He smiled and raised his hand to acknowledge the call of Stateline's bass player, Bruce Trent.

'Okay. Sorry folks. I'd better get back in there. See you in a while.'

The song they were working on today was one called *A Dream for Two*. It was a mid-tempo number which, Sylvia told them, had 'a really great hook-line'. Mostly they were going to be concentrating on the instrumental parts. But if it went well, they would start on the vocals too, which was where Sylvia came in.

The band had been recording the album on and off for the last two months, all the material having been written during a three-month rest following their last coast-to-coast tour of the States.

'I think they've got some really good songs this time,' said Sylvia. And she nodded rhythmically for emphasis. 'The last album was a bit disappointing. None of the band were very pleased with it. Especially Bob. He was depressed for weeks after it was released.' She lit a cigarette and continued. 'It was the record company. They were putting on the pressure for them to keep to their contracted "one album a year". And the band weren't quite ready. So in the end it was all a bit rushed.' She drew on the cigarette and exhaled two streamlined jets of smoke through her nostrils. 'They only perform one of the songs from that album now at their concerts.'

At around twelve-thirty, the door of the control room opened and a freckled young teenager, wearing a pair of blue-and-white-striped dungarees stumbled into the room laden with a mountain of plain brown bags, all obviously full. It was the signal for everything to stop. The band downed instruments on seeing the boy, and raced into the control room. It wasn't until the contents of these mysterious bags began to appear that it became clear to Sarah what was happening.

The sandwiches were enormous. Pastrami, corned beef, salami, roast beef and turkey filled them so copiously that the slices of bread outside them hardly ever got closer together than about three inches. Then there was a varied selection of canned drinks from Budweisers to Cokes. A cacophony of hisses could be heard as everyone seemed to pull the ring on the can of their choice simultaneously.

At about one-thirty the band resumed work. Sarah had to confess to herself that listening to the same tune being played over and over again for three or four hours, could begin to pall a bit. Especially when there were no vocals to make the thing a little more interesting. It was a catchy tune though. Nonetheless her mind began drifting off. Daydreaming again.

The time came for the band to add some vocals to the track they were recording. Sarah came back to earth with a start.

'This will probably take even longer than the instrumental parts,' Michael Cantello said as he turned his head towards Sarah and David, while continuing to expertly twiddle knobs and flick switches on the mixing console. The band had freed themselves of guitars and drumsticks, and were standing at a different set of microphones, singing and speaking into them so that Michael and Phil Stanton could check the sound levels.

Bob Carter was going to be singing lead on this one, so he had one microphone to himself. The other four members of the band were grouped in pairs around two other mikes to add some harmonies in appropriate places.

'Okay. Here I go,' said Sylvia, as she stubbed another cigarette out into an ash-tray already holding a mountain of lipstick-touched dog-ends. She jumped down from her stool and opened the two thick, heavily padded doors which separated them from the band, and padded in, bare-footed, to join two black girl singers standing by yet another microphone.

Another half-hour of technical preparation and they were set to go. The tape rolled, and the voices sang. The atmosphere was really beginning to come alive now, as the song actually began to sound like one, instead of a slightly monotonous, though pleasant, instrumental track. And as they repeated it time after time, Sarah found herself singing along with it, the words becoming more and more familiar to her.

This continued for about an hour, until, in the middle of one take, Bob stopped, waved his arms in the air for Michael to halt the tape, and said breathlessly, 'It's still not right, Mike. Let's take a break, huh?'

They all came trooping into the control room and sat around looking pretty dejected.

'Do you want to hear it?' Michael Cantello said sourly.

'Do we want to hear it? Are you kidding?' Bob sighed heavily. 'It was dead. Absolutely dead. That "hook" is supposed to lift the whole thing. It was like putting a lighted match into a bucket of cold water.'

'It sounded quite good to me,' said David enthusiastically. But it only brought a series of mutters and moans from the performers.

'Yes, I thought so too,' Sarah ventured. And she began to sing the catchy chorus and clap her hands to the rhythm still beating in her head. Bob turned to Sarah suddenly, his dejected expression slowly brightening and widening into a big, familiar grin.

'Hey, can you sing?' he said. He had a thoughtful glint in his eyes.

'Er . . . well, I used to be in the choir at school. But I didn't really follow it up after that.'

'Well, I think you're about to,' and Bob clapped his hands together with a rejuvenated enthusiasm. 'Okay everyone. Back in the studio. I think we've just found what was missing.'

Three more takes and it was perfect. The extra voice on the chorus had been just what was needed. When they'd finished the final version, Bob stood with his hands on his hips, nodded his head and spoke into his microphone.

'Ladies and gentlemen,' he gasped, trying to catch his breath. 'I think we have a hit on our hands.' Almost before he had finished his sentence the whole studio erupted. They jumped around, cheered and hugged one another. Unbounded euphoria charged the whole place. And enormous relief.

When Sarah returned to the control room David wasn't there.

'Oh, he said he was just shooting out for a can of beer,' Michael Cantello replied when Sarah asked where he was. 'I told him we'd send the kid again. But he said he wanted to stretch his legs anyway.'

By this time, it was a little after seven o'clock. Everyone in the studio was ecstatic. The atmosphere sparkled with joy and success. They were slapping each other on the back, kissing, hugging and laughing. Then the freckled youth who had brought in the sandwiches at lunchtime, poked his head into the control room, and told Sarah there was a telephone call for her in the office.

'For me?' said Sarah, surprised. 'Did they say who it was?'

The boy said no.

As Sarah walked along the short, narrow corridor, past walls adorned with signed photographs of famous rock stars, and gold and silver records in glass frames, she felt a minute charge of terror course through her. She walked into the empty office, and picked up the receiver that lay on the large, smoked perspex table.

'Hello.' There was no reply. 'Hello. Who is it?' But by this time, Sarah knew. And then the voice came. The same voice she had heard that evening, alone at David's apartment.

'I'm still here, you know, Sarah,' said the voice. 'Have you missed me?' Then a short muffled laugh. 'I haven't forgotten about you, Sarah. There is a price to be paid, and you must pay part of it.' He paused. 'With your life. Just like Penny paid. Paid for being a whore.' Then she heard the sudden click and the continuous dialling tone.

'Penny,' she mouthed silently. He had said 'Penny'. That name rang and echoed around her head. She heard him say it again and again. 'Just like Penny paid.' Much more than Penny's recent reappearances, the icy reality of those words plunged her back in time to that tragic day over a year before. Her insides twisted with the same anguish and abject misery she had felt then. But now she felt fear too. Cold and uncompromising, it emerged in little beads of perspiration on her forehead.

Now, standing in that large, elegant office, she felt alone in the world again, cut off from anything that resembled love, tranquillity and continuity. A vacuum where everything was dead or sterile. She stood there for a couple of minutes, numbed. Not really able to think anything. Then she returned slowly to the control room.

David was back, laughing and chatting with Bob. He looked up as she came in, and smiled.

'Who was it?' he asked as she walked over to where they stood, leaning against the sound-proofed window. I must appear natural, she thought. David certainly did. But then a psychopath would, wouldn't he?

. . . The girl Benson meets is Frances Selway. Pretty, English and in her early twenties . . .

Sarah did her best to smile and look relaxed.

'Oh.' She hesitated. 'It . . . it was Cathy. She was wondering what we were doing for dinner tonight. I said we were probably busy.'

'Of course you're busy,' Bob interrupted. 'You must

come out to celebrate with us. After all, we couldn't have done it without you.' He moved off to get the evening's festivities organized. Sarah glanced up at David. He was looking at her with a curious frown.

'Sarah, there's nothing wrong, is there?' he said softly.

Oh, how she wanted to believe the sincerity and concern on his handsome face. How could that possibly be false? But she just couldn't feel sure. And still she couldn't say anything. It would confirm nothing if she brought the whole thing to issue herself. If David were the culprit, he would certainly have some brilliantly devised explanation all worked out. And his strange game would still go on, tied in intricately, as it seemed, with the plot of *Call Back Yesterday*. No. She had to carry on waiting until something positive, but out of her own control, happened. She would just have to be alert, aware and ready for it when it did.

'No, I just need some air,' she replied. 'I haven't been outside since we got here.'

They went off en masse – all twelve of them – for a celebratory dinner at a fashionable Greenwich Village restaurant and stayed there for about four hours. Everyone got joyously drunk, including Sarah. But her reasons were somewhat different from those of the band. She didn't sip her cocktails, she almost gulped them down. It was the same with the wine. It was partly nerves, and partly intention. She wanted to get as drunk as possible, as quickly as possible.

'Hey, steady on,' David said to her, early on in the evening, before he too had submitted himself graciously to the general atmosphere of abandoned inebriation.

But Sarah couldn't help it. For tonight, anyway, she wanted to forget. And at one point in the evening it struck her that this was probably how alcoholism started. A desire to be lifted in a cloud of light-headed carelessness above and away from one's problems.

It worked but when Sarah awoke next morning, she felt

dreadful. The room seemed to spin round, slowly, uncontrollably. Her head felt as if it belonged to someone else, and her mouth was parched and sticky. David was already up. She managed to tear herself from the bed. Her body had wanted to stay there. But this head on her shoulders – whosoever it was – told her the best way to cope with her hangover was to do something about it. She staggered into the kitchen. David was sitting at the table, head in hands, massaging his temples. He looked up as she came in.

'God, I wish you wouldn't walk so loud,' he said with a pained expression. Then he squinted at her, as though trying to make a brave attempt at focusing on her face. 'Hell, you look as bad as I feel.' He beckoned her over to him. 'Come and have some coffee. It's strong and black.'

There was an instinctively agreed silence for a minute or two. Sarah sipped at the hot, steaming coffee. At length she broke the silence.

'One thing I can't remember, among goodness knows how many others, is how the hell we got home.'

'Don't ask me. I haven't the faintest idea. I guess they must have put us into a cab. Although, for the life of me, I don't remember paying for one.'

The silence resumed. Sarah felt as though someone was drilling through her head with a model of the pneumatic variety. David squeezed and rubbed his upper left arm, his face screwed into a weary, agonized contortion.

'You know, I keep getting these dull spasms shooting through my arms and legs,' he said. 'I've been getting them ever since I woke up.'

'It's probably alcohol poisoning,' came Sarah's matter-of-fact, unsympathetic reply. She wasn't really in the mood for giving sympathy.

'Thanks a lot.'

'Don't mention it.' Sarah poured another mug of coffee from the pot.

'I remember the wine and cocktails at the restaurant,'

156

David remarked, prodding the table clumsily with his fore-finger. He looked up towards the ceiling in an effort to focus his mind on the rather hazy recollections of the previous evening. 'Then I think we started on the bourbon at Bob and Sylvia's place. But after that . . .'

'After that, you threw up. That much I do remember.'

David looked up in surprise.

'Did I?' He smiled. 'At my age as well.'

'I think I'll go back to bed, and start again later on.' Sarah downed the last mouthful of coffee, which by this time was little more than lukewarm, stood up and staggered back to the bedroom.

FOURTEEN

David had received an invitation to attend the world premiere of the new Paul Newman film. It had arrived courtesy of World Pictures. The mysterious World Pictures whom David always spoke of as if they were the Mafia or something. Sarah had heard of them, of course. But she hadn't as yet managed to meet any of the executives of the organization, with whom David had fought and now won his long-running battle over the casting for *Chain Reaction*.

'You're invited as well, if you're good,' David had said waving the invitation in the air as though the ink were still wet, and he were trying to dry it.

The premiere was to take place two days after the drunken night following the recording session with Stateline. Although the invitation had come the week before, in their rush to cram as much into their last two weeks as possible, they had forgotten all about it. They had arranged to spend a few days in Boston, but the dates clashed. If they wanted to go to the premiere, they'd have to put the Boston trip off for a day or two.

On the morning of the premiere, David wanted to put the finishing touches to the short story he had been working on. Sarah thought perhaps she'd go and browse round Scribner's bookshop on Fifth Avenue.

'Are you walking?' David enquired absently, as Sarah was about to leave. He sat hunched over his typewriter, fingers poised for action.

'No. I think I'll take the subway for a change. I'm probably not going to get much more opportunity.'

David protested. He didn't like the idea of her travelling on the subway alone.

'Oh, don't be silly,' she scoffed. 'It's day-time. There are lots of people around. And besides, I was doing it all the time before I met you.' David reluctantly conceded. And she left him.

As she came out of the apartment building and made her way towards the subway, she reflected on how difficult it was becoming to act naturally in front of David. She was making an increasing number of excuses not to be alone with him. Yet there was an irony in that when she was alone with him, it was probably the time that she was safest. For him to murder her in those circumstances would be far too obvious. He would never get away with it. It was at times like this, alone, that she was in the most danger. But if she kept to where there were other people around, she should be all right.

David was being as loving and affectionate to her as ever. It was so difficult to believe anybody could contrive quite that amount of false goodwill. And yet she was doing it herself, to a certain extent. But, she suspected, not quite as convincingly as David.

If David was the threat, then, in a sense, she still had one card up her own sleeve. David had no idea that she had seen the outline for his new novel, the only thing that might point to him in any way. So he wouldn't necessarily know that she suspected him at all.

Sarah veered dramatically from moments when she half-expected him to pounce to times when he would make love to her with such power and authority and yet skin-tingling tenderness, that love seemed all there was in the world, and everything else was pure fantasy.

What was the reality? Still she was trapped, waiting for something to happen that would finally make it all fit together. Waiting.

It was while she stood on the platform at the 86th Street subway station, not far from the apartment, that she looked across at the opposite platform and saw Andrew Simpson.

He was standing fifty yards or so further along and didn't appear to have seen her. What could he be doing here at this particular subway station of all places? She thought of waving, attracting his attention. But no. That would be silly. It was best to let sleeping dogs lie. At that precise moment she heard the clatter of the train as it emerged from the tunnel. Its graffiti-covered carriages, a mass of swirling patterns and colours, ground to a halt in front of her. They had become an art form in New York. You could even buy books about them. The doors opened, and closed behind her, and the train lurched southwards.

Sarah and David were standing in the foyer of the R.K.O. on Broadway, chatting to George Fenster. George *P.* Fenster as he insisted on being known. The chief executive of World Pictures was a short, fat, balding man of fifty-five. His red, puffy face creased conveniently in a straight line just above his nose, just sufficiently for the two slits he had for eyes to see their way out of the squelchy, fleshy mass that surrounded them. No, he certainly wasn't a pleasant sight. And unfortunately he didn't have much else to redeem him. His voice was that grating sort of croak that made you want to clear his throat for him all the time. As far as his professional reputation was concerned, that was as tarnished as that of any major film company executive who regularly graced the gossip columns of the Hollywood rags. There was no way George P. Fenster could ever be considered a well-liked man. But he was a very powerful one, just about the most powerful in the film world. And most people were just plain scared of him. It made David's standing of his ground over the *Chain Reaction* controversy even more impressive. In fact David had confided to Sarah that in the end he felt it was the simple fact that he had stood up to Fenster which had convinced the man to concede.

'I honestly don't think he really gives a damn who plays the lead,' David had said. 'The irony is that it isn't any of my business anyway. I know they asked me what I thought. But that was specified in my contract. They never imagined I'd act on it.'

Fenster moved off to mix with some of the other guests. Sarah turned up her nose when he had gone.

'God, what a revolting little man.' And she shivered. 'He made me cringe.'

'Now you know what I've had to put up with all these weeks,' David muttered, looking around the room.

'Seen anybody else you know?'

'No, not yet, have . . .' He stopped for a second. 'Oh dear. Look who's heading this way. How the hell did he get invited?'

'Well, well, my children. Fancy running into you here of all places.' The unmistakable voice of Jonathan Peterson. And although David obviously wasn't too happy, Sarah was surprised to discover that she was quite pleased to see Peterson.

'We thought you'd gone back to England,' she said.

Peterson took her hand and kissed it theatrically.

'And go without saying farewell to you, my adorable little dryad.' He lifted her hand and took a step back to get a more complete view of her. 'You are, I might add, looking simply divine this evening, my dear.' And from the admiring glances cast in her direction since they had arrived, Peterson wasn't the only person to think so. Sarah was sporting a dress she had bought on the spree with Cathy. It was a subtle blend of pastel stripes, with a low v-neck, short sleeves and a pale blue tie at the waist. She had decided to make the most of her long hair, since she had made up her mind to have it all cut off when she returned to England. Also the heat wasn't as uncomfortable as it had been recently, and so she didn't feel the need to put her hair up. Peterson allowed Sarah's hand to drop and turned to David. 'And as for you, young Dent. I do believe it's the first time I've ever seen you wearing a suit.

161

I'm sure you won't mind me saying it looks quite ridiculous on you.'

'Thank you,' David grinned, his moustache thinning and spreading as he did so. 'That's the nicest thing anyone's said to me all evening.' He looked Peterson up and down, an amused smirk creasing his face. 'But, Jonathan, don't you think top hat and tails is going just a little bit over the top?'

Peterson stroked his lapels delicately between his forefinger and thumb.

'Rubbish, dear boy. Absolute rubbish. This is a grand occasion. We Brits have to show these scruffy colonials how to conduct such ventures. If we can't, who can?'

There was a break in the conversation as someone announced it was time for everyone to make for their seats. The three of them began to shuffle along with all the others towards the entrances to the auditorium. And before they parted to go and search for their respective seats Peterson said, 'By the way, I insist you both join me after this fiasco for a little night-cap.'

They arranged to meet outside the cinema when the film had finished.

Sarah thoroughly enjoyed the movie. It was a romantic comedy, something she was in just the right mood for. And Paul Newman, one of her Hollywood idols anyway, had given a superb, light-hearted, tongue-in-cheek performance.

Afterwards, they took a taxi with Peterson back to the Plaza Hotel.

They sat in the opulent splendour of the lounge of the Plaza and the conversation flitted around inconsequential topics before touching briefly on David's new novel.

'Presumably you've kept your admirable vow to yourself, and not revealed the subject of this proposed masterpiece to Miss Brownlow here,' Peterson said as he peered into his glass and shook it gently so that the ice clinked against its side. David looked uncomfortable. The edge of his mouth twitched nervously. He was obviously angry and made no attempt to disguise the fact as he snapped:

'Yes I have kept my "admirable vow" as you call it. And it hasn't been easy.' David glanced quickly at Sarah and then looked down at the glass in his hand. 'But I think . . . I hope that Sarah understands now.'

Sarah leaned across and gently squeezed David's arm. 'Of course I do,' she said. No, she didn't. She didn't understand David at all, but she couldn't tell him that. He had to believe she knew nothing about his next novel. It was her only advantage, her only clue to the next move in the game. She would give nothing away that might threaten that.

There was an awkward silence. David looked sharply at her, before getting up, and muttering something about more ice, leaving Sarah and Jonathan alone at the table.

Sarah felt immediately uneasy to be alone with Peterson again, even so temporarily. So much so, that she couldn't bring herself to look at him. She couldn't quite forget how awkward she had felt as they had sat in the Four Seasons restaurant. That knowing half-smile; the piercing, confident eyes. Something told her if she looked up now, she would see it all again. A repeat performance.

'Sarah.'

Now she would have to look at him. He continued in his low, velvet tones. But softer, more quietly. Without the contrived pomposity she was used to. 'I don't know what you know of me. Of my past,' he began. 'I expect all the stories from publishing's gossip circles have filtered through to you from David. It doesn't bother me. Let them enjoy their speculations.' Peterson swept his hair back from his forehead. 'I just want you to know that there is much more to me than meets the eye. I think perhaps you're already aware of that. And if you ever need a friend – or something more interesting . . .'

Sarah was hypnotized by the man's intense, mysterious

stare. And there was the smile again. Not a smile exactly. It was just the vaguest of expressions. Barely perceptible on its own, but together with those eyes, the whole effect had a subtle but disconcerting chill about it. They were caught in this silent spell for several seconds. Then David returned, and, as though someone had flicked a switch, the conversation slipped back to one of relatively harmless chatter.

But why had Peterson said what he said? And in such a disturbing manner. He must have realized that in such a short space of time, the period during which David left them, he wasn't going to be able to say much more than he had. And yet it seemed that he had no desire to. What he had said to her appeared to be all he intended to say.

And for the first time, she seriously countenanced the fact that the madman, the sinister-sounding maniac who was threatening her, might even be Jonathan Peterson. Though she had absolutely no idea of what could have provoked him. And how could he have known about Penny? The whole thing must be some kind of monstrous practical joke. Surely Peterson could not be the man. Yet how could she believe that David, David who said he loved her, who took such tender care of her, could be torturing her in such a cold-blooded way? The cat and mouse game she was embroiled in was becoming a living nightmare. She could trust no one, nor could she confide in Cathy or Frank. After her breakdown, they would only think she was cracking up again, and not to be taken seriously.

It made Sarah feel fleetingly alone again. She told David of Peterson's offer.

'Love, he's just acting up, making a pass at you again,' David said absently. His mind was on something else. He was attempting to teach himself to juggle. He'd seen a paperback book complete with three cuboid bean bags in the Barnes and Noble bookstore the day before and had bought it. Now he was standing in the centre of the sitting room, breakable objects duly removed from danger, en-

gradually close until her head dropped forward, and the shock of the sudden movement would restore her to a bolt-upright position of temporary alertness.

Now the cab was heading up Sixth Avenue towards Central Park. What was that? A girl on a street corner had turned to face her as the taxi sped past. For a moment she could have sworn . . . She must have dozed off for an instant, and experienced one of those split-second dreams. One block further. The next corner. A girl turned to face her as they passed. The same face? The same girl? Another block. Another corner. Again. Sarah was wide-awake now. As the next corner approached she gritted her teeth in expectation. Her heart thumping. Surely David could hear it. Yes, there was no doubt about it. Penny.

For the next five blocks the vision was repeated. The twist of the head. The long, flowing hair swishing round a fraction of a second later to momentarily obscure the inscrutable expression on the face she knew so well. It was like a team of dancers doing a well-rehearsed routine. Split-second timing. Perfection. Suddenly, she was no longer tired. Penny was back again. She glanced across at David. His chin was resting firmly on his chest. He was asleep.

. . . *Benson's good looks, and his effortless, convincing, yet completely false charm, combine to draw Frances to him* . . .

FIFTEEN

Just over a week to go. They planned to fly back to England on the twentieth, and that week was going to be mainly spent buying last-minute presents and saying farewell to all the people who had so warmly welcomed them. But Sarah was distracted. That most recent, repeated apparition of Penny had cast another shadow over their final week.

Her uneasiness must be apparent now, she thought. She was naturally quieter, less effusive. And David noticed, though his acknowledgement of her subdued state seemed very cursory. Surely if he really cared about her, he would be so tuned in to her changes of mood that he would show more concern over this current one. But he merely muttered things like, 'Mm, you happy?' when Sarah grunted some low-key response to a question he'd asked. He never asked her what was the matter. This made her even more anxious. She supposed there were two possible explanations. One was that, as a writer, he was so insular, so closeted with his own thoughts, so used to being on his own, that he couldn't expand his outlook sufficiently to really encompass someone else in his life as well as himself. Sometimes, when his thoughts were obviously far away, she felt distanced from him, excluded almost, from his world. The other possibility was that . . . well, she didn't even want to have to contemplate that again. But she had to. Supposing he knew exactly why she wasn't jumping about with enthusiasm? Why her brow would sometimes crease into thoughtful, worried furrows? And, of course, he still hadn't mentioned anything about the future.

Only one thing made her breathe easier. There were no more letters or telephone calls to further disturb her already unsettled tranquillity.

Henry Bloom gave them two tickets for the men's final of the Open Tennis Championships at Flushing Meadow. Traditionally Smithson's had tickets for each day of the tournament, which they handed out to authors and other important business contacts who happened to be around at the time.

It was an enthralling match – Connors versus McEnroe – on a divine day that reminded Sarah of English summers, warm but not oppressive. The setting too, brought back the taste and smell of strawberries and cream, and school outings at the end of June to Wimbledon. Home. She wanted desperately to be home. But the day out to Flushing Meadow, even if it was the connotations of England which had brightened her thoughts, had succeeded in lifting, temporarily, the new clouds of doubt and uncertainty.

For the rest of the time, days were spent shopping, and evenings socializing. Sarah said she preferred to look around for presents by herself. This was partly true. She didn't like tearing around shops with other people if they were looking for different things. But also she found herself wanting to be alone again. Not completely alone, of course. That was hardly possible on the crowded sidewalks of Fifth Avenue and the like. But she wanted time to reflect again, away from David's side. The evenings didn't allow her that luxury. Everyone wanted to take them out for extravagant dinners and to discotheques and jazz clubs. But as she darted in and out of department stores and jostled with tourists and lunch-time New York shoppers, she felt safe, and able to pinpoint her thoughts against the background of seething activity. And then there was the fact that David didn't really have many presents to buy anyway. He travelled abroad so much that his friends and family at home didn't expect gifts each time he went away. So while Sarah was out spending the last of her dwindling supply of dollars, David made a last attempt to try and visit all the people it was necessary for him to see before he left the country.

There were interviews, too, that had been organized by the public relations office at Smithson's. One was with *Time* Magazine which was to appear a couple of weeks later, and another was a live engagement on the *Johnny Carson Show*. It was funny how these things seemed to come all together, and right at the end of David's stay in New York. It was all such a rush now. But he was already too much of a professional to turn down the opportunity of such immense public exposure. He knew, too, that the more he was in the public eye, the more was the likelihood of his next novel being accepted, whatever it was.

In fact it was the day after the *Johnny Carson Show* appearance that Sarah met David for a light lunch in a small, intimate restaurant near the Rockefeller Center. Sarah had got there first and ordered a Campari and soda while she waited. David arrived three or four minutes later, red-faced and breathing heavily. He'd been running. He leant across the table and kissed her on the head, before sitting down opposite her. He was obviously excited about something.

'You'll never guess what,' he said, as he cursorily scanned the menu before him.

'What's that?'

He closed the menu, having clearly made his choice. 'Just after you left this morning, Henry Bloom rang. He'd just received a call from Martin Cranshaw, a producer for the Starlight Picture Corporation. Apparently Bloom had shown the synopsis for the new book to him weeks ago and he had shown a little interest. But for some reason, seeing me on the Carson show last night had made his mind up.' David lightly thumped the table with his fist. 'He wants to do it. Definitely. And you know what that means don't you? Bloom and Peterson are going to have to give me their full backing. Money talks. And there's no way they're going to turn down the possibility of the extra sales a film would bring.'

'Very nice,' Sarah mumbled. But her thoughts were elsewhere.

'Aren't you pleased?'

'I guess so.'

. . . What is Benson's game? Is it possible that he has actually fallen in love with Frances, contrary to the usual patterns of psychopathic behaviour . . . ?

Although Sarah was now quite eager to get back home to the slower pace and intimate smallness of England, she was still going to miss certain things about New York. In these eleven weeks she had almost become a New Yorker. She knew her way around as well as she knew her way around London. Her life had begun to beat with its rhythm. And although she did find that rhythm faster than she was used to, this only became apparent when she came across something which reminded her of England and its more ponderous approach to life, or her past which was still very much part of her.

But in the deepest recesses of her being there burned, unmistakably, the uncertain fire of expectation. Its flames leapt and danced randomly. Still Sarah waited, apprehensive, unable to dictate events, to take them by the scruff of the neck. She was powerless.

Bloom and his wife Marion took Sarah and David out for dinner, one evening, to Le Plaisir on Lexington Avenue. It was an extremely fashionable restaurant where, not only was the food superb and its presentation a delight, but you could hardly move for celebrities. Sarah noticed Jon Voight and Art Garfunkel at tables quite nearby. She decided that she liked Henry Bloom. She remembered having a soft spot for him when they had first met. But since then she had rather taken him for granted. And it was only now, when the end of the holiday loomed and she realized she might never see him again, that she was aware of herself warming to him. Although that charming, jolly exterior of his encapsulated a clever, talented man, there was nothing secretive or sinister about him. And he had no pretensions. That was his greatest strength.

The following evening was spent with Cathy, Frank, Bob and Sylvia. Its flavour was completely different to the previous one, and Sarah preferred it. She was with people closer to her own age, with interests and tastes in common with her. Mr and Mrs Bloom were very nice, but she couldn't imagine them being terribly *au fait* with the latest Rolling Stones album or the most recent crazy fads in dress and pastimes.

They began the evening at an inexpensive restaurant in Little Italy. Cathy chose it. It was one of her favourites. And cheap it may have been, but the food was excellent. They stayed there until about ten-thirty, managing to soak up six bottles of red wine in the process. Then they took a taxi to the Village Vanguard to catch the second set of the jazz saxophonist, Dexter Gordon. The Vanguard had a wonderful sleaziness about it. A tiny basement, to which you descended down a steep, narrow staircase, it could only hold about ninety people, who sat around rickety, circular tables smoking, drinking and listening. The air was hazy with smoke and the floor sticky with spilt drinks. But when the gangling Gordon came onto the stage, mumbled something quite unintelligible, and began to play, the atmosphere was so spiced with anticipation, you could almost taste it.

On the very next day, two days before they were due to leave, it happened.

She and David had stayed in bed until quite late that morning. David had slept through. But Sarah had actually woken up early, around seven o'clock, and lay tossing and turning, trying to get back to sleep. She knew she was tired but she couldn't get herself to drop off again. Apart from the things which had been worrying her for some days now, there was something else. Something she couldn't grasp with her comprehension for long enough to know what it was. It weaved and darted in and out of her thoughts with the speed and elusiveness of a frightened squirrel. She couldn't pin it down. Couldn't feel its presence properly. It was an atmosphere more than anything else. It meandered and floated, free of the confines imposed by reality, tangibility.

David stirred and groaned. He was beginning to wake. It was just after ten-thirty. He turned towards Sarah and rested his arm on her waist. But he still had his eyes closed, trying vainly to postpone the inevitability of a new day beginning. Sarah stared at him, a puzzled frown wrinkling her forehead. She chewed at the side of her mouth. He looked so innocent, so ingenuous, lying there. As if butter wouldn't melt in his mouth. But that didn't really signify anything. Everyone looked like that when they were asleep. How could she guess what secrets lay hidden from her behind that gentle, peaceful face? Realistically, Sarah knew there was no proof at all to support her suspicions. But there were no other candidates who could possibly know so much about her, or who could wish her such dreadful harm in this alien city.

Breakfast was quiet, almost solemn. Sarah didn't feel much like indulging in animated conversation anyway, and David didn't seem that concerned one way or the other. To Sarah the silence felt awkward, even frosty, but David appeared quite relaxed with it. She supposed it was her mood which coloured her interpretation of the atmosphere. It was strange the way people observed things like that differently, depending on their frame of mind. Eventually, it was David who unselfconsciously broke the silence which had until then only been dented by the occasional tinkling of a coffee cup as it was replaced on its saucer.

'What do you plan on doing today?' he said.

Sarah thought for a moment. What did she feel like doing? Well, with two days to go, she suddenly had the urge to go and soak up the bustle and noise of Manhattan again. She had done this same thing countless times since she had been in

New York. But as she had felt about Henry Bloom on that evening when he and his wife had taken them out to dinner, so she now felt about the pulse and vitality of New York itself. She had got to know it so well that she had long since taken it for granted. Tomorrow would be spent packing and preparing for the flight home the following day. Today was going to be her last chance to savour all the noises and smells and atmospheres of New York City. So she went, but on her own. David, who although he had idolized a good many aspects of life in the Big Apple, was obviously greatly looking forward to going home, decided he had seen enough. Bloom had invited him out for lunch with Martin Cranshaw, the producer who was so keen on filming David's new book, and he had accepted with alacrity.

As it turned out, once she was in the open air with the sun stroking her back and caressing her lazy daydreams, she was content to be alone. She wandered for miles, down Broadway to a little beyond the south-west corner of Central Park. Then east along 57th Street until she came to First Avenue, which she followed past the United Nations Headquarters as far as 34th Street, where she turned right and headed west across town again. The traffic rumbled, the police sirens wailed and the construction workers' drills juddered in short, sharp bursts of power. Wispy trails of subway gas rose like genies from the manhole covers. And if you stood in the middle of Fifth Avenue while the road signals were in your favour, and gazed northwards, it seemed to go on forever. Straight and wide and flanked by tall, sentry-like skyscrapers which appeared to meet at an apex in the distance. This was New York. It couldn't possibly be anywhere else in the world.

At around three-thirty she stopped by at a small café and sat by the window sucking languidly at the straw in her Coke and watched the city surge relentlessly towards the end of another September day. She thought about Penny. And she thought about David. And she thought about all the other things that had happened since she had been here in New York. But as she stared mindlessly out at what wasn't really anything in particular, but a kind of vague general impression, all those things seemed to have temporarily lost their sinister implications. Her thoughts were numbed by a drowsy feeling of well-being. She stayed there, entranced, for nearly an hour.

She got back to the apartment on Riverside Drive at about five-fifteen. David wasn't back from lunch yet. Where could he have got to? They had arranged to go out to dinner for the last time with Cathy and Frank that evening. David would want to have a shower before they left. And Cathy had asked them over for cocktails first, at around six or six-thirty.

Sarah took a quick shower herself, and changed into her baggy white trousers and a loose-fitting light grey sweatshirt. Her soft skin was still tanned, and her blonde hair still streakily bleached from the two weeks of continuous sun-bathing at East Hampton. Five forty-five and still no sign of David. She decided to leave him a note and make her own way over to Cathy and Frank's.

As she propped the note against the pale green, art-deco vase on the table, the telephone rang out. The sudden, piercing sound made her jump and momentarily rekindled the embers of fear which had, for a short while, become extinguished. It must be David. She picked up the receiver, and said 'hello'.

'Sarah, it's time.' The voice was so characterless, so cold, it didn't seem human. 'It's time for you to pay,' he continued. 'Are you frightened, Sarah? How does it feel to know that you are about to die? Are you sweating, Sarah? Can you feel the fear in your bones?' He laughed. 'Yes, Sarah, you whore. Penny's time came. She was a whore, too. And now it's your turn. I'm coming for you now.'

'Who are you? Why won't you leave me alone? What do

you want?' she cried, hearing the panic in her own voice. But as the line went dead, she knew exactly what he wanted. The police. Now, in the panic of the moment, surely she must call the police. This was it. It was about to happen. Now was no time to think about how improbable her story would sound. This was life or death. But by the time the police got here, she thought . . . Whoever it was, might be on his way up to the apartment now. No time. She rushed out of the door, and made for the lift. She didn't have to call it. It was on its way up. And as it came into view, through the thick, patterned glass doors, she saw the shape of a man. He was here. She bolted for the stairs and raced down them. Her legs didn't seem to be moving fast enough. Her brain was telling her body to go faster, faster. But her legs wouldn't respond. Four steps from the ground they gave out, and she tripped and fell to the hard, stone floor at the bottom. She got to her feet, but she had hurt her ankle.

She flung open the front door and ran into the street.

She entered Central Park at the 85th Street entrance. She knew the route across the park to Cathy and Frank's like the back of her hand. But it was gone from her memory now. Her mind went blank, and in a matter of seconds she was lost. And where the hell were all the people? It was only just after six. At this time it was usually sprinkled with men carrying briefcases, wearing light-coloured, light-weight suits, on their way home from work, or joggers punishing themselves with an early evening run before dinner. But they all usually kept to the main paths, and without realizing it, Sarah had strayed from those as soon as she had entered the park. She stopped and looked around her. No one. And then she heard footsteps. Rhythmic, running footsteps, distant at first, but becoming gradually louder. But where were they coming from? In which direction should she run? She was at a sort of mini cross-roads. She had three choices. She looked along the path ahead of her. There, about a hundred yards away was the figure of a girl.

She stood facing Sarah. The hair. The clothes. Without having to strain her eyes, she knew. She mouthed the name, but no sound came.

'Penny.' She looked round again quickly, as she broke into another limping run. He was there. Obscured frustratingly by the trees' shadows, but he was there all the same. She could just make out his vague shape against the dark shade of the thick-leafed branches. And she could hear the still-quickening snap of his shoes on the path, as he seemed to be closing on her. Her ankle was throbbing. But she just had to carry on. Her breathing became faster and she swallowed so heavily that it hurt her throat.

The cold perspiration of fear was beginning to soak through her sweatshirt. She looked up into the distance ahead. There was Penny again, still standing motionless. Still a hundred yards away from her. But her pursuer was nowhere near a hundred yards away. He was much closer. Perhaps no more than forty or fifty. His footsteps now reverberated as loudly as her own, but increasingly quicker. She daren't look round now. Just keep running. Why weren't there any people?

. . . Is it all part of some grim game he is playing? Benson seems confused in his own mind. The tension mounts as the reader becomes even more unsure of Benson's intentions . . .

Sarah seemed to be heading ever deeper towards the heart of the park, along deserted, winding paths that didn't appear to be leading anywhere. And always ahead of her was the silent, still figure of her dead sister, Penny.

'Please, someone appear,' she muttered to herself. She felt helpless now. Tears of fear and pain streamed down her cheeks, together with the tiny droplets of perspiration from her forehead. 'Penny. Penny, help me,' she sobbed, her voice croaking.

And then, suddenly, Penny was beside her, running with her, in one rhythm, as one person. Penny took her arm. She could feel the pressure of the grip. She was in Penny's hands now. She was too tired even to think. Behind them, she could hear the fast, measured breathing of her pursuer. He was very close now. Perhaps only twenty yards away. At any moment she expected to feel his touch too, and she braced herself. Where would it come? Her back? Her shoulder? Her head? Penny was pulling her now. Leading, guiding her.

Suddenly, she found they were emerging onto one of the main roads that traversed the park. They stopped, momentarily, at the edge of the road, and she felt his hand grasp her shoulder. She could smell him. It was a smell she knew only too well. But in that instant, the identity eluded her. She wrenched herself clear, without looking round. In that moment of supreme terror, she didn't want to see his face. Then she felt Penny suddenly pull her again, and they flew across the road. Blindly, she ran. Without purpose or responsibility. Penny was in control, and Sarah had submitted herself totally to her fate. It wasn't in her own hands. They darted in and out between the cars and trucks, which hooted as they shot past in both directions. As they stepped onto the pavement on the other side, she heard the screeching of brakes and the screaming of skidding tyres, followed by a sickening thud. She turned to the sight of a tourists' coach slightly askew from the direction in which it had been travelling. And twenty yards further ahead lay the crumpled heap of a human being. She stared at it for a few seconds, and then a thought struck her. She looked around her. There was no sign of Penny whatsoever. She had vanished.

Then as cars began to stop and their drivers got out to see what had happened, Sarah walked slowly, very slowly towards the prostrate figure in the road. 'Please, don't let it be David,' she muttered under her breath, as she approached.

The people who had stopped were muttering to one another. She heard the coach driver say to someone, 'Man, he just ran right out in front of me. I didn't have a chance.'

Another car door slammed.

'Sarah.' She spun round. It was David. She could hardly believe it. 'Thank God.' He ran across from the yellow cab he'd been travelling in. Around them there was chaos. The traffic had come to a halt, and police and ambulance sirens sang their whining songs of panic and emergency.

Together they walked on to the ring of people that surrounded the supine figure on the ground.

'Oh my God,' David muttered as they gazed down at the man. Blood trickled thick and slow from his mouth, nose and ears onto the road, and collected in small, globular pools. And there, staring up at them were the cold, lifeless eyes of Andrew Simpson.

SIXTEEN

Sarah and David spent the whole evening at the police station. There was a lot of explaining to do, and the detective conducting the investigation insisted that he interrogate Sarah alone.

By ten-thirty she was getting quite tired, and not a little irritable. This wasn't helped by the policeman asking seemingly pointless questions like, 'How can you be so sure this was the man who was threatening you? If you knew him, perhaps he was running after you because he wanted to say "hello".' The man must be a complete idiot, she thought.

They finally left the police station soon after eleven o' clock. Now she would have to explain it all to David. And he had a bit of explaining to do himself. He had telephoned Cathy and Frank from the police station and told them roughly what had happened. They offered to come over to Riverside Drive, but David thought it was best to leave it until the next day.

'I just can't understand why you didn't say anything,' David said, throwing up his hands in a helpless gesture. He had made them both cups of coffee, which stood steaming before them as they sat at the table in the kitchen.

It was time for it all to come out. Sarah took a deep breath.

'David. I'm going to tell you things that you don't know. That I've kept from you, I suppose.' She looked at him, her face pleading for understanding. 'But there are reasons why I've kept them from you, which will become obvious as I go along.' She took a sip of her coffee, and stroked her hair back from her face.

First she revealed about her trip to Bridgeport, and Andrew Simpson.

'I know we made an agreement about those couple of days,' she said. 'But I want you to know everything now.' She paused. 'Nothing happened there between us. You must believe that.' David nodded and Sarah went on.

'You remember when we first met. You asked me if I had any brothers or sisters and I said no?' David nodded again silently. 'Well, in theory that was true. I haven't. But I did have once. A sister. A twin sister. Her name was Penny. We were identical twins.' Sarah went on to relate something of their lives together. How close they had been. How happy.

'What happened?' David almost whispered. Sarah held up her hand.

'Just a minute,' she said. 'Can you work out the exact date you saw me on that road in Essex?' After about a minute David finally arrived at April 16th. Sarah sighed heavily and began slowly to relate the events she had long since tried to erase from her memory.

It was a sun-soaked, surprisingly warm spring Saturday, and while Sarah went for a three-hour horse ride, Penny decided to bicycle to the Braxtons' at Little Sampford. Philip and Lucinda Braxton were a young couple whom the two girls had got to know very well over the years. And whenever they felt like calling on them, either together or individually, they could always be sure of a warm welcome. This usually included a glass of Philip's latest attempt at homemade wine. And for all his effort there hadn't been an attempt yet that had been particularly successful. It was a standing joke between them, but Philip took all the leg-pulling with an amusing and good-humoured resignation which endeared him all the more to Sarah and Penny.

But Penny had never made it to the Braxtons'. She hadn't made it back home either. It was just before eleven o'clock in the evening that Sarah's father decided to call in the police. It was just after four o'clock the following afternoon that the body was found. It hadn't been a pretty sight for the farmer who had stumbled across it while repairing the hedge which divided his land from the Saffron Walden to Finchingfield road on the other side. The full extent of the injuries had never been revealed to the Brownlow family. But it had been no straightforward rape and murder, if such a thing could ever be called 'straightforward'. This was the work of a crazed man, hardly a man at all. More a wild animal.

It was seven months later that the police caught him. Or thought they had. The evidence was very insubstantial. And although the man had been charged and the long, laborious trial process had been cranked into action, it was beginning to look as though public outcry had panicked the police into arresting the first vague suspect that came along.

'And it happened on April 16th,' Sarah concluded. She paused. 'April 16th *last* year.'

There was a stunned silence, broken eventually by David, as the implications of this shattering revelation began to dawn on him.

'Jesus Christ,' he said. 'I don't believe it.'

'It's true, I assure you. And it has also become more and more clear to me over the last couple of months, that it wasn't me you saw on that road earlier this year. My memory was one of the things affected by the shock. That's why I wasn't sure at first. But then it became obvious.'

Sarah went on to tell of Penny's apparitions.

'But this is all absolutely incredible,' David said, shaking his head. He looked down at his now cooling coffee. 'Because I've got something to own up to now.' He told her of his synopsis for *Call Back Yesterday* and how that chance meeting on the Saffron Walden – Finchingfield road had sparked off the idea. 'It sort of festered around the back of my mind for a few weeks. And then some kind of shape began to emerge.' He stopped and reached across the table for her hand. 'I wanted to tell you about it. I really did. But I just didn't know how you'd take it. It's pretty morbid, I know. And you'd have been sure to make the connection and probably think . . . well, goodness knows what.'

A perfectly reasonable explanation. She knew there would be now. But this was a whole night of explanations; revelations; confessions. And she still had one more to make.

'David, I know about the storyline for your new novel.' She stopped and slowly ran her fingers through her hair. She really was feeling very tired now. 'I think you were out seeing Fenster, or maybe it was Henry Bloom, I can't quite remember. You left the folder with the synopsis out on the table in the other room.' She sighed heavily. 'Oh, David, I know I shouldn't have looked at it. I wasn't going to. It's just that you had been so mysterious about it, and I'm afraid my curiosity got the better of me. As it turned out, it would have been best if I hadn't seen it. Because, you see, it seemed so uncannily close to what really happened, that when the note came and phone calls started . . . Well, you can imagine what I was thinking. Incredible as it seemed, it looked as though, not only did you want me dead, but that you had killed Penny, too.'

David moved his hand across, placed it upon her own, and squeezed it gently. Then he poured himself another cup of strong, black coffee. 'Yes, I remember putting the thing away. I suppose I just assumed you hadn't looked at it. After all, you never said anything about it.' He leaned back in his chair until it tipped onto its two back legs, stretched his arms out in front of him and yawned. 'I still can't believe it,' he said. 'It's all so uncanny. Like something out of a Hitchcock movie.'

'Yes, I thought that. At times it seemed so ridiculous, I didn't know whether to laugh or cry.' Sarah downed the last inch of coffee in her cup. It was cold and tasteless.

They bought the engagement ring at Tiffany's the following afternoon. Where else? It was a magnificent sparkling cluster of ten tiny diamonds, set in an oval on a bright, white gold band. And buying it at Tiffany's was an experience in itself. Sarah had wandered into its hushed, opulent interior before. But it had only really been to sample the atmosphere, so that she could say she'd seen it. She'd never dreamed that she would be buying anything like her engagement ring there.

They had postponed the flight home for a further day, and Sarah had telephoned her parents to tell them the news. They were suitably ecstatic and Sarah felt as pleased for them as she was for herself.

The evening was spent with Cathy and Frank at Maxwell's Plum, as had been arranged the night before. This time it was a real celebration. Sarah was a little sad that the dinner signified a farewell. But that was inevitable. She felt a particular affinity for Cathy and Frank. Not just because they were family, or because they were such great people. They had been a kind of theme running through these last three months or so. They were there all the time. And even though she hadn't confided in them that much, it was the knowledge that they were around, quietly caring, concerned. It may well have kept her from cracking up altogether. But there was no danger of that now.

But there was still a further surprise to come.

Next morning, a team of policemen and pathologists went to Simpson's house and their findings had been quite spectacular. In the locked room which Simpson had told Sarah was his storeroom they had discovered what amounted to a shrine, dedicated to Simpson's estranged wife, Margaret. Simpson's story of his wife's drunkenness had been just another lie. The police had found the walls of the room adorned with giant blown-up photographs of the woman in her early twenties. She had long, straight, blonde hair and a slim figure. Piles of her clothing were littered across the floor.

And there were her letters. Letters written by Margaret to Simpson before she had married him. The outpourings of a woman apparently deeply in love. And in a separate, unmarked envelope they had found her last letter to her husband. Written after three years of marriage, she told Simpson what an utter bore she had eventually found him, interested only in his 'stupid little watches'; what a failure he had been as a lover, never satisfying her as she had expected he would; telling him how blind she had been not to realize what a terrible mistake she was making. Finally, the blow that had put paid to their marriage – the news that she was leaving him for another man. It had been a bitter attack on Simpson, full of taunts and insults, the last, wild lashing-out of a bitter, unhappy woman.

When the search moved to Simpson's bedroom, beneath the floorboards they had found several more items. There was a scrapbook, in which there were numerous cuttings from both English and American newspapers, concerning a number of brutal rape and murder cases in both countries over the previous few years. One such cutting had reported Penny's murder. Each cutting was accompanied by a blurred photograph of the victim as she had looked when alive. Each woman had been blessed with beautiful, blonde flowing hair. And in every case, the photograph had been savagely disfigured.

The police computers turned up the fact that – with the exception of Penny's apparent 'murderer' – in every case, no arrests had been made.

In the same box which had concealed the scrapbook, the police had discovered several diaries, covering the years since Margaret had deserted him. Initially the diaries were full of disjointed, vicious ramblings, about Simpson's planned revenge on his faithless wife. But gradually, the tone of the diaries changed. Margaret had been weak. She had been misled. She had followed the example of her sisters under the skin. She was blameless – but other women must pay for her mistakes.

The entry for April 16th of the previous year had read: 'Another one. She struggled quite a lot and bit me before I managed to punish her. Drew blood, the whore. But I punished her – punished her for Margaret.'

On April 17th: 'Saffron Walden a dead loss as far as the antique business is concerned. The whore's bite is causing me pain. Turning nasty. Have to do something about it.'

The entries in the most recent diary had also been illuminating: 'The girl beside me today on the flight back – I thought it was the Brownlow whore. The shock almost destroyed me at first. Then I discover her name is also Brownlow – from the same area. Can only be sisters. Thought I was seeing a ghost. Rude and capricious at the airport. What can you expect from a whore?'

David had been mystified why Simpson had not attacked Sarah when she had turned his proposition down. But, as Sarah explained, he had no way of knowing that she had told nobody where she was. He couldn't afford to take the risk.

'The whole thing gets more unbelievable all the time,' he said. 'Why can't I get away with plots like that one?'

He held Sarah tightly to him, love and concern written all over his face. Then he bent his head and kissed her.

She and David talked of the future. He would go ahead and write *Call Back Yesterday*, while she completed her final year at Cambridge. Then they would marry the following June. But David made it clear that he wanted her to have a career of her own. That it was important not to lose sight of their individual identities.

And surely now that the danger had passed, the future was assured, and she was happy, Penny would rest in peace. Sarah supposed that Penny's visitations hadn't just been warnings from the other world. They had been so close when she had been alive that they often knew instinctively what the other was thinking and feeling. Happiness and sadness, contentment and dissatisfaction flowed unhindered between them. So that they shared each other's sorrow as well as joy. And now in death, as she had in life, Penny would be as content as she had, during the past weeks, been troubled. Everything was perfect again.

EPILOGUE

'*Pan American flight PA2 to London Heathrow, now boarding at gate 15.*' *The voice from the public address system echoed round the airport building.*

'*Well this is it, I suppose.*' *David stood up, nearly knocking over his bag of duty free booze as he did so.*

'*Careful now,*' *said Frank, catching it as it was about to topple over.*

Now they all stood. Sarah, Cathy and Frank too. None of them could look at one another. Sarah, David and Cathy stared at the floor, while Frank gazed over to where the other passengers were slowly filing out of the lounge and showing their boarding passes at a desk in the glass-sided corridor.

'*There isn't really anything to say,*' *said Cathy. Sarah leaned across and pecked Cathy on the cheek. Cathy responded with a big, emotional hug. Then they all hugged together in one amorphous clutch and promised they would see one another next year. Either here in New York, or back in England.*

They inched along the corridor. Tears cascaded down Sarah's face, and all around them people seemed to be afflicted with the same problem. Nearly everyone seemed to be sniffling or sobbing or shedding silent tears of sentimentality. David showed the boarding passes to the uniformed man at the desk. And as he did so Sarah turned one last time to wave to Cathy and Frank. There they were, noses almost touching the glass and clouding it with their breath. Who was that behind them? That boyish shock of silky, blond hair. The strong, angular jaw. Those mysterious, intent eyes that seemed to know so much. Jonathan Peterson. And was that a smile on his face . . .?

NIGHTSHADES

A major new series of original paperbacks.
Nightshades are contemporary novels for women –
a new kind of love story.

FONTANA PAPERBACKS

Contemporary Romances

Once a Lover £1.95   **Diana Anthony**
Set in New York and San Francisco, *Once a Lover* is the
moving love story of Lainie Brown, a young artist, and
Jean-Paul Vallier, a blinded sports superstar. Then he
regains his sight and Lainie fears she will lose his love. But
she learns painfully and joyously why she is so worthy of
Jean-Paul's enduring devotion.

Celebration £1.50   **Rosie Thomas**
Bel Farrer, a wine columnist, was a high-flying career girl.
But beneath her glittering professional appearance was a
vulnerable heart. Both the titled aristocrat bound by an
ancient code of honour, and the reckless, carefree playboy
claimed her heart and she had to make a choice.

Perfect Dreams £1.75   **Carolyn Fireside**
The world of high fashion, Hollywood and the jet set is
the backdrop for this rich love story. Gabrielle Blake, a
photographer's model, is independent, intelligent and lov-
able. Among the rich and famous men who fall in and out
of Gaby's life is Terry Baron, a young journalist who
finally rescues her when her career collapses. But is it too
late for them to rescue their love for each other?

Perhaps I'll Dream of Darkness £1.35   **Mary Sheldon**
In this compelling and beautifully written story of love and
obsession the lives of a teenage girl and a burned-out rock
star entwine fleetingly — with disastrous results. Probing
deeply into her characters' lives, Mary Sheldon creates a
portrait of frustrated passion that leads to tragedy, and
captures both the grace and terror of obsessive, idealistic
love.

FONTANA PAPERBACKS

Fontana Paperbacks

Fontana is a leading paperback publisher of fiction and non-fiction, with authors ranging from Alistair MacLean, Agatha Christie and Desmond Bagley to Solzhenitsyn and Pasternak, from Gerald Durrell and Joy Adamson to the famous Modern Masters series.

In addition to a wide-ranging collection of internationally popular writers of fiction, Fontana also has an outstanding reputation for history, natural history, military history, psychology, psychiatry, politics, economics, religion and the social sciences.

All Fontana books are available at your bookshop or newsagent; or can be ordered direct. Just fill in the form and list the titles you want.

FONTANA BOOKS, Cash Sales Department, G.P.O. Box 29, Douglas, Isle of Man, British Isles. Please send purchase price, plus 8p per book. Customers outside the U.K. send purchase price, plus 10p per book. Cheque, postal or money order. No currency.

NAME (Block letters) _____

ADDRESS _____

_____

_____